The Moment Thief

Andrew Thurlow

Andrew Thurlow

To Will, for inspiration in your silence

Contents

Also by

Andrew Thurlow

The Colour of God (2023)

The Dream Photographer (2025) – Part One of the Dream Vision Trilogy

Chapter One

The Hot Ticket

People who knew, knew that unlaced shoes are preparation for disaster.

After much thought, as a solution to combat such things, Douglas had developed a habit of looking down.

A lot.

Just a quick check every so often, possibly accumulating into spot checks that totalled about thirty minutes per day. So you could say it was a problem, unless you were Douglas, who saw it as prevention worth the time.

That particular habit may have wrapped up his personality, but only on a singular plane. Douglas was so much more complicated than that. He should have been prancing around confidently, master of his domain, lord of his knightly realm, but the people in his life he was supposed to trust had made sure he didn't get the time for that.

The first was his wife, Adrie.

She had been spending a significant amount, some of it on him, not that he had asked for it. Douglas wished she had understood, or at least listened, when he had said they needed to slow down a little until he could complete the launch of this new business. Not only did he not need the additional financial strain, he definitely didn't need whatever it was she was purchasing.

But while many in his field listened to Douglas, the people around him knew him better, apparently.

His business partners were another bunch who just knew what he needed.

He needed control and to have control he needed to do everything. Particularly Big Sam seemed happy that Douglas thought he was in charge. Sam would turn up for the fun stuff, the overseas junkets supported by the government or the talk fests, anything that didn't involve actual work. Sam would hit the casinos until late and then turn up for coffee, chat to a few prospective clients and then wander off for an afternoon sleep. In contrast Douglas, organised everything to get there, setup the tech, manned the exhibit, did interviews, consolidated, noted down any glitches, answered any proposed modification customers may want. Then, when it was all over, tore it all down before they moved on to the next show. Big Sam said he didn't understand all that techie stuff and Douglas knew the reason for that was he never looked and never tried to learn.

Douglas ran the team in the office too, sure he had help from his Technical Manager Paul, who was a saviour in no uncertain terms, but Douglas needed to be all over it, push where pushing was required. For a while he hoped he might get some structural help from Johnno, after all Johnno ran a labour company so he was kind of in that same sphere of work. Johnno had been over-committed, and when his wife Tracey started to have some heart issues, he backed out almost completely.

Douglas would just have to handle it, they said. No plan, no backup, just get to it.

So he did, and up to the point he met Amber, he was all work.

Amber joined the company in May and it took a few months but eventually the two of them just fell into each others arms.

You could only talk about it for so long before you wanted to taste.

They fell and tasted and travelled and whether anyone saw it or not, they were as together as together gets without involving other people. Douglas was so together he was ready to pack the whole thing in with Adrie. Amber had broken up with her regular guy but his spectre still lingered, Douglas really couldn't work out why, maybe she just needed time to decompress.

What did all this do to Douglas? Well between the three a.m. conference calls to the office, the seven a.m. starts to set up sales meetings and the grind of a full day, he also had to catch up with the four jobs in the office he actually did. Regularly he had to interface with government, send out information to potential customers and just trying to keep in touch with what the rest of world was doing.

Douglas was tired. When Douglas was tired he slept and when he slept he dreamed. He didn't wake up rested and ready for the day. He woke up exhausted, drained, rattled and thin. Not that he was thin, because he ate and drank a lot. Douglas didn't dream food, he dreamed about being lost, being alone, longing for companionship.

Amber had started with the company in Sales. Douglas desperately needed the company to get on the path to generate sales. His tech research and development was great but the market was not full of early adopters so he needed to get people on the path of trials, wider trials and then early sales before full adoption. Something he could show financiers. So Amber had been bought on to help him.

In true Douglas style after entering his life, she entered his dreams. Then after so many coffees, so many conversations and so many texts, to his surprise, she entered more than his dreams. Douglas' relationship with his wife, Adrie, was pretty stale, maybe not dead, but it had no spice. Amber was all spice.

So he didn't so much jump as pivot. Amber came with him on company trips instead of Big Sam. Big Sam was busy with other business so he didn't mind. Adrie didn't ask anything about the business.

No one in the office seemed to notice when two rooms became one, and then the rooms moved from the Holiday Inn to an old German palace. Twice the price but only one room. Douglas controlled the finances, the government submissions and realistically he was out on the road a lot, so if he wanted comfort he took it.

Amber loved it. To start with.

The relationship grew and burned and then tempered and cooled and was ready to move to another stage. It was about this time Douglas had his first few days off work, not that anyone except Amber noticed. He just couldn't lift his head, couldn't focus enough to turn his big brain onto the tasks of the day or even into putting on his shoes and tying his laces.

The headaches were debilitating.

First, he took a few days off. Then he missed a few social shareholder functions. He let Big Sam and Johnno get those ones, but then he missed a customer engagement and then a sales trip. Amber hadn't been going on that one, and his head had hurt a lot, so he just let it slide and substituted someone else in.

Once he felt better, Douglas saw a few doctors, then optometrists, then ophthalmologists. He changed his diet a little, but nothing seemed to fix his headaches. The small amount of time he had for himself, he spent with Amber, or getting near Amber, or returning from seeing Amber.

Things with Amber took more of a turn when he moved the business focus from Rotterdam to London. That step got everyone's attention, except Amber. Douglas explained it was for her, that he wanted to be with her. That didn't get the reaction he had expected, she supported him but wanted the move to be something he did for him. Douglas was a smart man but he really didn't understand. As his health deteriorated more and Amber tried to create some distance, ironically in a perfect twist of fate Adrie walked back into focus again, knowing just what he needed.

She organised a trip to a GP which lead to a referral to a cardiologist, and his problems were finally discovered. High blood pressure, with a strong probability of a stroke or a heart attack. Douglas had lost his mother, grandfather and other family members to Aortic Dissection so he needed to take this news seriously. His cousin had died at forty nine and Douglas was just pushing up past fifty, so that time was now.

The medication he wa given had a most profound effect, most noticeably on his dreams, Douglas went places and experienced things so extensive and so amazing, he felt he needed to take notice. The huge landscapes, elongated time frames, the bizarre constructs and highly unlikely scenarios made him wonder what it was all about. To make it worse, living those moments in his dreams seem to make his blood pressure worse.

Amber would message him from time to time. They even hooked up a few times. Douglas wasn't sure, but he thought Amber was on the way out, just hanging around to draw the last breath from what they had together, physically. His disappointment was written all over his face but in consolation Adrie made the difference with a gentler demeanour and a better attitude.

Did she know about Amber? How could she not.

This had a further affect on his dreams, wandering around these huge worlds for hours, bleating Amber's name in the darkness, sifting through endless hotel rooms looking for her, talking to inane and uninterested hotel or café staff, or just people lingering around wide, empty streets or yawning, gaping spaces. Sometimes the spaces looked outdoors until he hit the wall.

Both in dreams and in reality Douglas hit the wall.

His first stint in hospital was short, just five hours. He had never moved so fast through the queue of waiting people at the hospital. Fifty year old man complaining of headaches and chest pains. Straight to a quiet corner, doctor by his side in five minutes, stabilised, tested, checked, tested again, medicated, observed and cautiously released with a note for his GP.

His GP referred him and the cardiologist increased his testing regime and his medication.

The rest of the world waited for Douglas to return to work.

Amber had chosen that moment to resign and move on, from both the company and Douglas. Well, she gave the company nothing more, but she met Douglas a few more times in his apartment. Just to squeeze every last drop from him.

It was hard to give up as that part of the relationship hadn't reached the end yet. If anything it was still rising but the rest of her life was closing in and Douglas suspected she had a more suitable, younger, less married suitor who was knocking on her electronic door.

Adrie kept on with her life in Rotterdam but Douglas went back to work. But from that moment his passion was gone and that to him was everything. How does a man who has lived his life on passion move on from that. Everything about Douglas's life had screamed passion from his relationships to his music, his pursuit of education and knowledge, his work, his travel. His whole life had been about passion and now emotionally trapped by one woman and emotionally depleted by another, ignored by friends, used by partners, scrutinised and judged by family. Douglas felt bound, blocked, tied and controlled.

His return to work was unheralded and he went back to the coal face as quickly as he had left it. Reports, summaries, responses, technical verification, submissions, account balancing, share holders, accountants, certifiers. It took about two months before Douglas went back to the hospital but this time in an Ambulance.

His blood pressure was acute. The doctor increased his medication again, which made him listless, bordering on groggy. In a blessing Douglas just couldn't see, he recommended rest, starting with a few days in hospital. Adrie was there quickly. She sat by his bedside quietly at first, before her phone rang.

"Babe, The Dream Photographer," she said to her friend Janna, "Supposed to be amazing. The clarity of his images from dreams are meant to be next level. I was thinking I could frame it, make it a talking point in that area near the balcony."

Douglas wasn't asleep but he also wasn't very interested. Adrie had a habit of taking on whatever crackpot thing was on trend. She went through stages, grabbing at things, spending his hard-earned money on whatever piqued her interest for a few minutes, before moving on to the next shiny thing.

"I found out about him on Reddit," she ploughed through the word Reddit like it was foreign soil. "Mostly he just sees students. I don't know why I got in, but apparently it's a hot ticket."

Douglas opened his eyes slightly, "I have to go, babe, call you back later, Douglas is awake."

Adrie held his hand. "You OK, pet?" she asked with genuine affection.

Douglas nodded. "Some water please," he croaked.

Douglas let the cool water trickle down into the parched valleys of his aching throat.

"Where am I?" he asked.

"London," Adrie replied gently. "Hospital, pet. You had a heart attack." Douglas closed his eyes.

"From the doctor's account to me, you might have died," Adrie was gentle but to the point. "Working too hard, no doubt."

Douglas left his eyes closed now fully resigned to his fate.

"You just rest there. The doctor will be along soon," Adrie said, holding his hand loosely.

Douglas lay there, awake but not really zoned in. The water wasn't enough, but he couldn't find the enthusiasm to lift his head to take more. He remembered being in a meeting with a potential customer, the customer had been frustrating, using the spectre of additional functionality before committing to trial his device as it was in its current state. He just wasn't going to put up with it.

'Get on board here and the additional technology will come in time, but not now.'

There was nothing else on the market to compare, but you just can't pick and choose in the highly regulated electronics safety market. He had defended that stance many times to keep the product stable, not that Big Sam or Johnno listened. They always wanted changes without realising the gravity of those changes.

Taking himself through those events, Douglas remembered the conclusion of that conversation, followed by the searing pain in his chest, like someone was behind him slicing into him with a sharp star picket. That was the end of the memory. It must have been bad if he had blacked out.

The doctor arrived and gave his prognosis, suggesting a few days in hospital and then home for a few months' rest. Douglas nodded dutifully, knowing the repercussions of that and how very, very unlikely that was to happen. Adrie added her full agreement, she needed him alive.

After the few days in hospital, Douglas took his leave of London, and of Amber, and headed back to Holland. Big Sam and Johnno seemed more worried about who would do what while he was convalescing, rather than how he was feeling. Douglas could hear the echoes of them trying to remind him of his responsibilities.

'We need you back, fighting fit,' Johnno had coughed in his deep, casual voice. 'We can't run the place.' Sam had admitted. 'Shareholders depending on you.'

The forward pressure had been just what Douglas didn't need.

Douglas and Adrie had a large house in the wealthy suburb of Kralingen in Rotterdam. The house was everything they needed and more. Douglas just needed rest, which involved bed for a week, some physio for a month, and no work for probably three months. Adrie was doing her best to look after him, and Douglas appreciated the effort. Things hadn't been the best between them for a while, so it was nice to see she still cared. He hadn't ever stopped loving her. The thing with Amber had some love and might have gone somewhere, if Amber had any real interest, but he knew she didn't. Douglas was like that, he needed to receive to give, or at least meet halfway. That was unlikely, as Amber knew he was married, so she would never trust him fully. She might have said she did, but he knew she didn't, or he knew he wasn't trusting her until he knew she was trusting him.

So what is love without trust?

Adrie showed love, trust, loyalty, commitment, the whole nine yards. In return, that was what Douglas should have given.

***

Adrie was beside herself.

She busied herself around the house, tidying and cleaning Moving things to a new location and then cleaning and tidying again. She wanted to make everything perfect for Douglas. He spent such a small number of hours in Rotterdam and an ever dwindling number at their home. She wanted him to feel comfortable.

"Yes pet. He's home with me now," her voice reached a medium-pitched squeal, not ear shattering but higher than normal. "It was most certainly a close call Juul. I could have been organising a funeral. The doctor was very clear."

Adrie rattled about with some photo frames removing the dust and then changing where they sat on the sideboard to make them look more orderly. Juul's responses came through very loud like she was talking from inside a wind tunnel.

"I know," Adrie said.

"Yes, you are one hundred percent correct my lovely," her replies confirmed that Juul was also worried.

"Yes, it's great I have him here instead of having to sit in smelly old London."

"Yes, it's booked in for this week on Thursday." Adrie said excitedly as the conversation finally turned to her Dream Photographer appointment.

"Quite amazing apparently, but all under the cloud of non disclosure so I can't tell."

"Yes, I'll tell you all about it after, actually Janna, Elsje and Fleur are all meeting me for a coffee on Friday at 10am, you should come too."

"Great, I must fly pet. I have so much to do before Douglas wakes up. Ta ta, see you Friday."

It was a cold day in Rotterdam. Who would believe there was snow last night. Snow in Rotterdam.

Adrie had the inside warm but not too stuffy, fresh and breathing, so it made everything easier for Douglas. She had cooked his favourite split pea soup with some crunchy bread. She really wanted everything to be perfect.

He worked so hard for everything they had, she didn't want to lose him. In her heart she respected everything he did and was looking forward to when he could retire and they could travel some more. She had plans for them to go on Cruises to Asia and maybe even the USA and Hawaii.

Right now she was happy to have him home. She spent such a lot of time perfecting their home, she wanted him to enjoy it, but he spent so much time on the road. This new product had really dragged him into some dark places, where he had nothing but work on his plate and on his mind.

Adrie's phone rang again. The callers name 'Saskia' flashed up.

"Sass," Adrie said joyously.

"Yes, I know pet," she replied to whatever pearl of wisdom flowed from her friend.

"Lucky to be alive they said."

Adrie danced around the living room while she listened to Saskia tell about a friend who had a similar problem and how everything worked out fine. If you can just make him give up work.

"Well, it's a little early for that but let's see," Adrie replied.

"Yes, it's tomorrow," she replied to Saskia's inquiry about her appointment. "I am bit nervous to leave Douglas alone. But its just four hours and he has been sleeping twenty hours a day so it should be OK."

Adrie adjusted the throw rug she had meticulously placed on the sofa in an effort to make it look less perfect and more natural.

"Yes. I think it's the medication. It's a bit of a wait and see. His next doctor's appointment is next week."

"Yes. I know," Adrie sat on the sofa to try the new rug configuration and adjusted herself to take the form of the sofa. Her figure was slim but not as slim as it had been in her youth and her flaxen hair now shone with just the odd strand of grey. She liked it and decided against colour, looking to age with grace.

"Really," she said happily, talking freely, and living the life of her friends as they did hers. She was happy with where life had bought her. When dinner time came and went, and Douglas hadn't stirred, she thought better of disturbing him and put the meal she had made for him in a container for consumption when he was ready. She satisfied herself with a glass of wine, a nice Australian unwooded chardonnay, thinking she would eat when he did. After a second glass and another phone call, this time from Malou, she settled in to watch another episode of her favourite Netflix drama 'Women of the Night' before heading up to bed.

Douglas was still, but she could hear his breathing as she slid silently beneath the covers and turned her back to him to sleep. Sleep came fast but didn't hold as she felt Douglas move around uncomfortably. She wasn't used to him being home so her usually sound sleep was easily broken.

"Are you OK pet?" She whispered in the darkness.

"Fine," he said gruffly, "just need to move, spent too long in one position."

Adrie looked at her phone which she kept beside the bed. It was four a.m. Once Douglas settled, sleep returned quickly.

Adrie woke up as Douglas turned his body sharply on the edge of the bed and placed his feet neatly into his slippers.

"I just can't sleep any more," his voice was raspy. "I really need some water and maybe something to eat, but nothing to heavy."

Adrie glanced at her phone. It was seven a.m.

"No problems," she replied. "You should wait here or in your study arm chair and I will bring something in." She rubbed his back for a moment to help his with the blood flow. "I made some split pea soup last night or I can prepare some *beschuit* with cheese and meat or jam and chocolate spread.

"Thanks Adrie. Maybe a little soup and some bread. I will be in the study." Douglas got up stiffly and moved slowly. Adrie quickly gathered herself and her phone and headed downstairs.

The place was cold so she moved straight to the central heating controls to warm the house. She prepared the meal quickly and put on some coffee for herself. She wasn't sure if Douglas was allowed coffee so just got him some water. She put it all on an ornate tray she had bought just for occasions like this, and took it upstairs.

Douglas was in his study but at his desk not on his relaxing chair.

"Really pet, you need to rest," she chastised him lightly.

"Just checking urgent stuff and forwarding it on. I am finished already, let me move over there."

He moved slowly like he was gripped at the ankles by clamps joined together by poles. He was not so old and Adrie had never seen him quite so constricted. He carried his phone over to the chair and sat while she fussed around the tray.

"That looks perfect sweetheart. Thank you." Douglas said smiling sweetly.

"It's OK," she replied and moved to the chair on the side. "I put on the central heating but it seems to be taking a while. Are you warm?"

"I'm fine. It's perfect." Douglas said taking a large mouthful of water and swallowing painfully.

"The doctor said you should avoid the stairs for a few days, so best you stay up here," she reminded him gently. "I will put together another tray when I go out so you can graze through the day, eat when you like, sleep when you like." She stared at him with her best look of concern. "Please, no work. OK pet," she said turning her head sideways hoping to get another angle on his response.

"OK," Douglas said

"I have an appointment at eleven a.m. with the Dream Photographer," Adrie reminded him. "I would cancel but he is like a one off, no repeat and I figure you will be sleeping for most of it." She emphasised the urgency in her own way. "It's OK isn't it pet?"

Douglas had managed to get down three spoonfuls of soup and a piece of bread.

"Yes of course. I think I'll sleep through that time but can you wake me up when you're back please."

"Of course," she said, "you should rest."

She took the tray downstairs to put away and began her day with a coffee and some *Beschuit*, meat, cheese and fruit juice. She looked in on Douglas before she went to shower and got ready to go out. In the shower Adrie thought carefully about the outfit she had laid out to wear and promptly changed her mind, truth be told she had changed her mind three times. She had taken a lot of different outfits out and scanned through the remainder of her extensive wardrobe. True to form she changed her mind several more times, before finally settling on something that was similar, but not exactly the same, as what she had chosen in the first place.

She checked in on Douglas who had finished eating and was asleep again. She sat quietly completing her morning routine of makeup, skin care, hydration and then changed again before realising that if she wanted to be on time to the appointment she should really leave the house soon.

The Dream Bakery was walking distance on a nice day or she could cycle, if she had chosen a different outfit. Anyway a walk would do. It wasn't a nice day but instead it was a cold, glum Rotterdam day, the brilliant Azures and bright oranges were in hibernation and had given way to scattered pastel blues, sketch greys and the occasional puff of white cloud.

The walk was uneventful and Adrie took it at a medium pace. She was on time so didn't need to rush. She enjoyed walking or cycling around Rotterdam, she couldn't think of anywhere else she would rather live. She thought through her things to do after this appointment to make Douglas comfortable, top of the list was to bake him some of his favourite pastries.

She could see the Dream Bakery ahead. She knew the building from many years ago, it was always such an eyesore, she was surprised when she got the address on the email. It must have been a few years since she walked passed. They had clearly done amazing things restoring the fascia to its original look while modernising the building. It's previous foreboding, disaster area look had given way to sleek lines and a professional glassy feel.

Adrie went to push the door and found it locked. Surprised, she knocked on the glass before noticing a doorbell on the side, which she promptly pushed.

She heard the door lock click open and pushed to be admitted.

***

Douglas woke up feeling very groggy.

He could hear Adrie downstairs talking to one of her friends. She had left him some snacks and drinks beside the bed but he was tired of being in bed and he really wasn't hungry, even though he hadn't eaten much in the last few days. His mind turned to what had happened while he had been knocked out. But first things first, the smell emanating from his body was disgusting, he needed a shower.

The bathroom was brilliantly white and super clean.

He hated hotel showers, they all had little quirks and foibles, unmaintained shower heads popping water left and right, inconsistent or insufficient flow, with water either blasting hot or freezing cold. But this bathroom was cared for by Adrie and she would have none of that. It was one of the joys of being home.

After the shower, given what he had been through he actually felt pretty good. Still a little weird, but on the road to recovery. Douglas stood behind his desk, not willing to commit by sitting, but he fumbled with the keyboard and his phone to complete a two-factor login.

Seven hundred and four emails. His heart twitched slightly and he breathed in, unable to get the air he needed until he coughed to kick start his body to life. He scrolled through the list looking for anything important or anything from Amber. Unfortunately there were too many of the former and none of the latter. He checked his phone and found a few voice messages mostly from Big Sam who seemed unable to use text messages or email so always wanted to talk.

Also nothing from Amber. Douglas was about to send her a message when Adrie came in.

"Hey, no work pet," she scolded.

"We need to keep your heart relaxed, just for a few more weeks."

Adrie walked over to his desk and gently grabbed Douglas by the shoulders directing him to the bed.

"Not the bed," he cried sheepishly, faking that it was a dreaded instrument of torture.

"OK, the chair then." Adrie redirected him and Douglas sat gently and sighed.

"So nice to be home, that shower must be the best in the world," he said in a heartfelt compliment. "My bones ached and my skin felt clammy until that beautiful shower."

"Yes, pet. I look after our home, it needs to be the best," Adrie smiled.

Douglas sighed again, 'I'm alive' he thought, giving thanks for small wonders.

Adrie's phone rang and she dropped today's newspaper next to Douglas before answering.

"Hello Sass, my babe. Yes it was amazing, let me tell you," she blew a kiss to Douglas and headed downstairs.

Douglas picked up the paper for about ten seconds before discarding it on the sideboard.

'Useless waste of trees,' he thought.

He took up his mobile phone and scrolled through the messages. He ignored Big Sam but replied to the message from Johnno that he wouldn't be able to get to anything for a least a week and wouldn't be back in any kind of rotation for a month or two. Both still seemed more concerned with his ability to work than his health.

Douglas could hear Adrie chatting away to Saskia about her dream appointment. It was hard to know whether it was interesting or not as every conversation had a high level of excitement with Adrie, especially when she was on the phone to her endless stream of friends. He checked the football scores, the basketball and looked in on some investments before opening his e-book reader and settled in to read for the evening.

Adrie was right, he should relax.

"I'll tell you all about it later over a glass of wine or two," Adrie walked back in and gave Douglas a disapproving look. He turned around his tablet to show he was reading a book and her scowl changed to a smile.

"Good boy," she touched him gently on the cheek. "A few days at least pet and then you can get back into it slowly." She smiled at him sweetly, "I know you have a lot on and Big Sam and Johnno are useless, but that nice man Paul can take care of things for a few days and Kit has all the technical stuff worked out."

"Sure," Douglas nodded. "You're right."

Adrie sat on the bed still looking concerned.

"Tell me everything, about your appointment." Douglas said surprising Adrie.

"Well," she said, "you just wouldn't believe how accurate his pictures are. Actually showing me a photograph of what I had dreamed while I was asleep. He said first time is just general but next time he will tailor the process a bit more around my dream, you know the one I keep having that seems to be in the future and just wont go away."

Douglas smiled and nodded, he had heard about that dream so many times. Some sort of erotic thing that Adrie had cooked up.

"So he measured your brainwaves?" Douglas asked.

"He had this cute white spacey looking hat, it was a bit tight," Adrie replied.

"Interesting," Douglas added, "and what, you just slept and he read your brain patterns and produced a graphic image? That's some tech."

"First he showed me some pictures and played some sounds maybe for five or ten minutes until I fell asleep. Nothing sordid, just chairs and cups and shells and fish and whale noises." Adrie couldn't remember all the images or sounds.

"So what was the picture?" Douglas enquired, "Can I have a look?"

"My dream was a beautiful tea party by the seaside. He said he would email it tomorrow after the 'high resolution rendering' was done." Adrie emphasised the technical words to help Douglas understand.

Douglas smiled. "So he seeded your dream with stock images, that's very cool."

"Yes, that's it," Adrie smiled a bright gleaming smile, her veneer teeth shining in the glow of the modern chandelier lights that hung above the bed.

"I am excited, next visit is next week," she added.

Chapter Two

The Winter of our Discontent

Joost was out on his morning walk again but his time he was seriously rugged up.

Who would have believed they would have snow?

He took his usual route but at a more brisk pace to warm himself up. The thin layer of white would soon turn to mush and he wanted to see the park looking bright and clean.

Joost took the final turn into the park and was amazed. The winter wonderland presented in front of him was breathtaking. He took a few photos and continued his walk. His spirits were very high as he trotted on through the park but on his last turn he spotted someone sitting on the bench.

Was that Lem?

As Joost got closer, he noticed Lem had some snow on him. He rushed over to check on him.

Lem was frozen solid.

Joost put in a call to emergency services and was quickly surrounded by ambulances and police cars. He was taken to one side and asked to wait, but it was very cold so he asked if it was alright if he moved around a bit to stay warm. The officer was very nice and said if he liked he could walk around the park but please stay close until the detective arrived. Joost walked to the entrance of the park and back again and then again. On his third walk back the nice police officer offered him a cup of tea which Joost gladly accepted. He used its warmth to raise the temperature of his fingers.

After about twenty five minutes a large truck arrived, which had a heated room for Joost to sit and wait in, an hour after that the detective also arrived. Joost watched him survey the scene and look over Lem from a window at the rear of the truck. The detective spoke briefly to the nice police officer who pointed to the truck, the two started walking towards Joost. The detective was a large heavy set man, tall in a dutch way but broad shouldered more in a Germanic way. Joost was taken by his gaze, which was intense. He pondered that such a gaze might be a true reflection of the soul.

"Good Morning father, my name is Wim Hummel and I am the assigned detective in this case." Wim spoke strictly, emphasising to Joost that this was important through his tone. "Thank you for assisting us with our enquiries."

"Yes, of course," Joost replied. "Anything I can do please just ask."

Wim paused and rested his intense gaze for a moment considering Joost carefully and relaxing his frown to a sort of a quarter smile.

"I understand you knew the deceased, Lem Forth." Wim read Lem's name from a small notebook.

"Yes," said Joost. "I was more friendly with his Aunt, but when she passed away I tried to help Lem, more as a community spirit thing than anything else. He was a difficult man so I really didn't do very much."

"What do you mean by that?" Wim had returned to his higher level of intensity, not aimed at Joost but more to convey the further importance of his words.

"Well," said Joost. "He was a funny character, gruff, opinionated, self consumed. Very much a loner."

"Was he part of your church congregation?"

"No," Joost replied. "His Aunt would attend, but I don't think he has ever been to church. Certainly not in my time."

"Right," Wim noted something down in his note book. "So why do you think he is here in this park?" The question took Joost by surprise.

18

"Well, he just lives over there." Joost pointed toward Lem's apartment trying hard not to state the obvious.

"Right." Wim looked a bit perturbed that he hadn't been told any of this earlier. "Does he often sit in the park?"

"Yes," Joost replied. "I just saw him sitting here last week. His apartment is quite small and I would often see him and his elderly Aunt out to get some air in good weather."

"Yes," said Wim, "and before that?"

Joost stopped a moment to think. "Well since his Aunt died just twice, the other day and the day after she died. He was distraught as you can imagine."

"So not often just a few times," Wim made a change to his notes and looked up with his quarter smile at Joost.

"Yes," said Joost "I suppose."

"That's great. Anything else you think might be helpful."

"Yes," said Joost "The manager of the apartments is called Michael. You can contact him by pushing the manager button near the entry. No need to break in, Lem should have his keys on him. I helped him to get in once and he promised me he would carry them with him."

"Thanks father," Wim said warmly. "Do you have time to come with me to the apartment? I am not sure what I am looking for but if you have been in there before maybe you can see anything untoward or missing."

"Sure," Joost had nothing else pressing. "Did you want to go now?"

Wim considered carefully. "Can you give me fifteen minutes to wrap things up outside?"

"No problems," Joost replied.

Wim turned and quickly made his way outside to join the nice police officer. The two had a quick discussion and Wim went back for another inspection of Lem's body, finding some keys in his jacket pocket, as Joost had alluded to. He also grabbed Lem's wallet and dropped them both in an evidence bag. He returned to the truck and showed Joost Lem's shiny half heart fob. "Any idea what this might be? Is there an other half?" Wim said in hope.

"I don't know," said Joost. "Lem had no friends or girlfriends that I know of. I am pretty sure he went to school here. He didn't seem to spend a lot of time in the community without his Aunt."

"OK, great." Wim looked in the wallet and saw over five hundred Euros. "A lot of money for a loner," he pondered out loud.

The two men exited the truck and walked briskly out of the park towards Lem's apartment. It was cold and the two kept a solemn silence on the walk. On arrival Wim took the keys out of the evidence bag and opened the door. Joost walked in first, Wim behind him.

Everything looked as it did last time Joost was in Mollie's apartment. Maybe a little more untidy as he didn't expect Lem was a big cleaner.

He turned to Wim. "It looks like it did last time I was here."

"Thanks father," Wim looked resigned to have to do this the hard way "What did he do, this guy, to have five hundred Euros in his wallet."

"Oh, Lem didn't work if that's what you mean. I would say it's his Aunt's money," Joost said in a matter of fact way.

Joost watched Wim look around in Mollie's room and found some bank statements and her journal sitting by the computer. He wiggled her mouse and the computer came on showing the bank account on the desktop.

"Right, maybe I will start by seeing where this money came from." Wim steered Joost to the door, "Thank you for your assistance father, you have been most helpful."

***

Wim had arranged time with the branch Mollie had kept her account. He found CCTV footage from the time of the withdrawal and noticed Lem went straight across the street from the bank to the store across the road. When he went out he noticed it was a coffee shop and he went in. The man behind the counter looked shifty, Wim was sure it was all in the eyebrows. In his defence the shifty guy did remember Lem coming in and having coffee and a muffin then leaving in a hurry. Wim questioned him on any friends and the shop attendant said he was alone but one of the regulars seemed to know him.

Jez was not happy when Wim knocked on his door. He really had enough Police problems without being presented any more.

"I am looking for information on Lem Forth," Wim said very formally. "I would appreciate anything you can help me with."

"Late again Lem," Jez replied quizzically. "Wow I don't see the guy for like years or decades and then I see him for one time and now I have the cops at my door."

"So you knew him," Wim asked.

"Knew him, know him, not really," Jez replied. "We went to school together and he was a drop kick but then I saw him the other day at the coffee shop." Jez looked around nervously. "I was a bit blown when I saw him, I tried to, like, you know, put the past in the past but then he ran off. I don't know, maybe I made him feel nervous. He was always a strange guy. What's the problem anyway?"

"I am just making some routine enquiries," Wim followed the police line perfectly.

"Ja right," Jez had heard that line before. "So he's in some trouble right."

"He is deceased." Wim said in a very straight tone.

"Oh bummer," Jez said. "He was OK, bit nerdy, bit weird, that's a shame."

"Do you know anyone else who might have any information on Lem or his associates."

"Nah," Jez wasn't being difficult he just didn't know. "Just his Aunt. She would know she was on him like glue."

"She is also deceased," Wim replied.

Jez looked surprised, "Oh snap. That's so bad."

Wim gave Jez his card and asked him to call if anything else came to mind. Before leaving he headed back to Lem's apartment and pressed the 'manager' button at the entrance. Michael was his usual bustling self but calmed down a lot when he realised it was the police and Lem was dead.

"He just kept to himself," Michael said "I try not to get too close to the tenants."

"OK, understood," said Wim. "Do you have any CCTV here?"

"Just one camera on the front. You can have the footage if you like. I will put it on a USB stick for you, would you like to come to the office while I do it?"

"Actually can you bring it to Lem's apartment. I have something else to check there."

"Sure. It will take twenty minutes or so to copy," said Michael.

"Great, thanks," said Wim walking off towards Lem's apartment.

He opened the door using the keys from the evidence bag and went straight in to the back towards the computer. He sat down in front and wiggled the mouse to wake the computer up. He opened the email and saw that Mollie had been doing some work with her employer.

He checked his notebook and noted that she had done this after she was dead. He looked closely at the emails from some time ago and then more recently and deduced that Lem had been doing the work since she passed. He moved to the calendar and noticed a few appointments Lem had at a place called the Dream Bakery.

Wim hunted around a little bit more until Michael returned with the CCTV footage. He checked it on Mollie's PC and happily returned to the station with something to work from.

***

Eugene scoured the Rotterdam news looking for any word on Lem's death.

Nothing!

He was sure the body would be discovered very quickly but he knew the Police often didn't release anything unless they had to. This was potentially not suspicious, so maybe it would go unnoticed by the wider community and be listed as just a heart attack in the park. He resisted making any attempt to compromise the local police network. The consequences of discovery might lead them right to him and double the suspicion.

The appointment with the new subject, Adrie, had gone well that afternoon. She was quick to respond to his email, compliant, cooperative and responsive. He had the process fine tuned for the basics and her seaside picture had come out perfectly. He needed to make it look like business as usual, so she was back next week and he had another guy in tomorrow.

"Report on the secondary system replacement," Eugene said impassively. He had started to put some plans in motion.

"System Update at thirty one percent, estimated completion at zero two hundred tomorrow." Daaisi was running three different primary tasks at the moment. Using almost fifteen percent of her Dream Bakery CPU and eighty two percent of her cloud CPU. "The high quality render should be complete soon, would you like to inspect the render before I email a link to Subject 260."

"Yes," Eugene had modified the render application to give a lower quality quick look which took five to ten minutes followed by a longer render which could take six or seven hours.

Eugene had also started planning to modify the Dream Bakery running systems to remove all stored data into the cloud. There was some replicated data that ran locally but afterwards it was scrapped in a cloud bin or torched completely. He wanted nothing left here if he had to go, no logs, no caches, nothing. Eugene had spent the morning in the storage area and his private area subtly preparing. He had a minimal bag of clothes, a suitcase for tools, the latest version of the dream interceptor and various tech gear. He wanted to be ready in case the police tied him to Lem's death. He knew there was no explaining what he had done and if they got past his door he would be locked up and no chance to get out. From his early interactions with the less salubrious people who purchased his software, Eugene had contact with a network of agents in a few specific countries. These were countries with relaxed law enforcement that can be persuaded to look the other way. Given the pending doom, he had quietly renewed some of these contacts to open up possibilities.

In preparation he had also made a call to have a private plane on standby at Antwerp airport which would pick him up from Haamstede airstrip about an hour away and take him anywhere. He could make the call from his car and by the time he got there the plane would be ready to whisk him away. Haamstede had no terminal, no staff and most importantly no camera's. His first thoughts were just outside the European Union but it would probably be better to head straight to South America. He had accounts and money, so such an escape was not outside his capability. If he left now and the police came calling, he would be an immediate suspect and that could cause future trouble. If they found nothing and let it go, he might get a single visit and then case closed and he could continue his work for a while longer before exiting gracefully.

The one thing Eugene had not done was slept, and he needed it. The other tasks Daaisi was working on included a complete hardening of all systems, and a removal of any systems within European Union boundaries. Eugene was pretty sure it would be a tough intrusion but closing any open ports except a control port and only opening what was needed when it was needed would make it tougher. It might slow performance but that was worth it to him. He could make some other changes later, when a more permanent location was arrived at.

"Render displayed on your monitor for approval, Eugene." Daaisi's deployment of Paige's vocal print melted over his tired body. He missed her sorely, what would she say to him now?

The render was of a perfect beach scene with a lovely tea party set up. White sand, turquoise water, crystal blue sky, deck chairs, towels, shells, everything that was in his package plus her own spin of a red and white table cloth, perfect crockery and cutlery and of course some pastries in a high tea setting.

"Approved. Send that to the test subject." Eugene sighed.

He needed to sleep.

"I will be taking some rest. Set the security system protection mode to maximum."

"Yes Eugene, I will lower the temperature in your private quarters to an optimal sleep level."

Eugene took the clandestine elevator up to his apartment on the first floor and fell dejected onto the bed. He lay fully dressed on the bed decompressing before he fell into a deep tormented sleep. A dream ensued of him running on the spot, followed by another dream of being trapped in a maze, followed by another of being caught in a confined dark space whimpering. Was that his mother? He squeezed opened his eyes in the darkness and lay for just a moment.

"Lights on," he said gently.

The lights came to a standard level.

"Any security incidents to report?" he asked.

"No Eugene," Daaisi replied calmly. "There have been zero incidents. You have been asleep for ten hours and there has been no contact except for a confirmation email from Test Subject 261 Bran Achterberg. The appointment is confirmed for eleven a.m. The current time is eight a.m."

Eugene felt like he had not slept. He got up robotically and headed for the bathroom, knowing that a shower and a coffee would fix his physical condition but the rest from here, he must leave to fate.

Chapter Three

Of Old Friends and New

Bran arrived on time and his appointment proceeded without issue. His picture of the seaside was stormy and grey possibly a reflection on his true state of mind as his seed pictures and sounds had been the same as Adrie's. The furniture was dishevelled and the beach littered, the sky grim but the pictures were very similar.

Like the same place with one picture taken in winter and the other in summer.

Eugene was enjoying his second coffee with Bran who was asking what it all meant.

"Well each subject gets a series of seed elements," Eugene explained. "From those we can direct your dream a little but certain elements have to come from within you, especially those without direction."

Bran nodded a certain level of understanding.

"The weather comes from you, you have aged the furniture but that furniture is from what I provided, you have added your own slant on the scene which is different from what others may add or you may potentially add on a different day. This is a snap shot and over a series of snapshots we can get a very good indication of the impact of life on your dreams."

"You mean of dreams on my life," bran replied.

Eugene moved his hands in a this way that way motion.

"So I should come back?" Bran asked.

"If you feel it's something you want to pursue. There are two paths you can take, if you have a recurring dream I can help you to picture it and try to understand it. Alternatively we can just run with my standard packages like this and with your consent I can show you comparisons with others who have also given their consent."

"... and you pay me to do this?" Bran clarified.

"Yes Bran and I'll make you coffee."

"The coffee is gold and the money would help. I am happy to share my results with others and see their results too."

"All under the NDA though Bran, you can have a high resolution copy of your photograph which I ask you not to copy or share electronically with anyone and other people have their photo which remain theirs."

"... and yours," Bran corrected.

"Yes," Eugene conceded "and mine. I get them all, that's the deal."

"Sounds great," Bran gave a thumbs up, "when am I next up."

"Next week same time if that's OK with you. We need to leave some time between sessions and I have some other people slotted in between now and then." Eugene could see Bran was in, maybe just for the money, but that didn't bother him now.

"OK great, thanks for the coffee. See you then. I can find my way out."

Eugene stayed in the kitchen and enjoyed the remainder of his coffee. The appointment had gone very well, from here he just needed to keep Adrie, Bran and maybe a few others attending to keep any suspicion low.

"Arrange appointments with two more test subjects, starting anytime they have available in three weeks. Make them afternoon sessions."

"Yes Eugene," Daaisi replied.

"A message has arrived on your personal social media while you were talking to Subject 261, Eugene"

"Really," said Eugene sarcastically. "Do I have personal social media? Which app is that?"

"You have a personal Reddit account which, earlier in this project, you used to verify the forums operation. It was never closed but earlier in the year you authorised me to monitor other personal accounts so you weren't disturbed when they wanted you to be, just when I thought it was appropriate, as I just did then."

"Who is it from?" Eugene was straight to the point.

"Will-I-used-to-be." Daaisi replied, "there is no surname, just the quadra-hyphenated first name. There is a strong possibility this is not an actual name as it doesn't adhere to any formal naming conventions from Australia, Canada, USA, UK or even Europe."

"Yes Daaisi, it's fake. You can call him Will, he is a school friend of mine. What does the message say."

"In town, party time." Daaisi read the words very flatly, without a meaningful tone.

Eugene smiled.

"Respond with an encrypted one touch link to a picture that shows this address in the centre but flip the picture horizontally. Include the text 'Dreaming' on the message." Eugene knew many people wouldn't know how to read that, but Will would.

When Will arrived the next day, Eugene was in the storage area, stripping a few parts away from old units and adding them to a secondary suitcase he was preparing. His plan was to leave them both in storage lockers on the way to the airport but if time was of the essence he could leave one and come back for it later.

"The person at the door refuses to identify himself Eugene. He just says you will know."

"Put the video feed to the storeroom monitor," Eugene said impatiently.

"That's Will, admit him to the ground floor. I am on my way down."

"Yes Eugene," Daaisi said coldly.

As Eugene walked toward the servery he could hear Will ferreting around in the drinks fridge.

"Gene Genie," he said like he was starting a game of hide a seek. "Where are you baby, come out come out wherever you are."

"Wilberforce." Eugene said as he entered from the hall. "Where have you been all my life."

The two embraced as Australian friends do, with strong pats on the back deployed in a manly way.

"Nice digs mate," Will commented. "Where are you hiding the chick on the intercom?"

"AI" Eugene replied. "Say hello Daaisi."

"Hello Will-I-used-to-be. Welcome to the Dream Bakery, my name is Daaisi."

"AI, you're shittin' me, that's so realistic." Will's expression was genuine disbelief.

"Vocal prints from an Ex." Eugene smiled.

"That's definitely not healthy, looks like I have arrived just in time." Will raised his eyebrows meaningfully.

"So what are you doing in Rotterdam?" Eugene asked.

"Mate, long story. Let's get a few more of these and I'll tell you," said Will reaching into the fridge for another Grolsch.

"Couple of slabs in the kitchen, leave those there or you'll break something. What's this?" Eugene pointed to a roller suitcase that Will had bought in.

"Got a couch I can lob on?" Will asked, as the two made their way down the hall. "Wow this'll do" he said running into the Interview room.

"What happens in here?" He said, wiggling his hips.

"Ya knob," Eugene said. "Kitchen is this way. You go first. What ever happened to Juliette?"

"No tying this Romeo down," Will laughed. "This is a nice setup mate, must have cost you a bomb. Are all three stories yours?"

The two sat for hours, they only drank a few bottles of Grolsch before Eugene showed Will where the whisky was stored and they caught up on six years of being apart. Eugene thought recounting his life was suitably sketchy but next to the tale that Will weaved, he was a model citizen.

Will thought, without doubt, he had a few warrants out in Australia, so he hadn't been back for a few years. He got out on a sailboat through Indonesia with a few legit crew, used a fake British passport to get past the Indonesian authorities and made his way up through Malaysia and Thailand. That was all fine until someone double checked and threw him in a local jail for using false documents. He managed to get out by using some money he borrowed off a mate to bribe the Police and quickly headed for Cambodia, flying out of there to the Philippines where he hung for a few years. After some fairly shady deals went wrong in Cebu he had managed to get to Tunisia and get in with some Italian pleasure seeking locals who got him back across the Mediterranean to Italy, from there it was all overland to Eugene's doorstep.

Will's story took most of three hours to tell and to keep it clean he cut all the tricky corners.

"Where to now?" Eugene asked.

"Well, Genie. I was hoping I could hang here for a bit, catch my bearings. As far as I know, nobodies after me here. Should be nothing international everything I did just created local chatter."

"Daaisi can you check if Will here is on any Interpol lists," Eugene said slurring slightly.

"Facial recognition and bio-metrics show no match," Daaisi confirmed. "I would need a full name and any known aliases to verify a correct match against law enforcement lists."

Eugene raised his eyebrows.

"You have got to be kidding me," Will burst out laughing. "She is amazing."

"This one you have to tell your name to, your real name." Eugene poked Will in the chest with a smile.

"It's been a while," Will grinned.

"Henry Masterford Wilbur," Will said with a smile draining his remaining whisky and holding up the bottle to show Eugene it was empty.

"Take your pick mate, the best of Irish in the front and some well aged single malts to the back."

"There is no known match for that name in the Interpol database. I have found information in Australia and the Philippines. Would you like me to display it on the screen Eugene."

Eugene eyeballed Will cautiously.

"No, I know him well enough."

"So you have heard and searched me, what's your deal buddy?" Will opened his eyes wide and stared long and hard at Eugene to get the effect he wanted.

"Yeah. I did some interesting deals around some financial software I was developing. Used it for a while then sold it to some super shady guys who gave me bitcoin just before it exploded. Enough to send some to my Mum and pop the rest into this place and some research I'm doing on dreams. I call it market research." The two both laughed. "I try and stay under the radar."

"Good call," Will touched his glass to Eugene's.

"*Proost.*"

"So where do those sweet tones of Daaisi's come from?" Will asked.

"That's Paige, a London based Chinese girl I had a thing with, ended a few months back, make that a year."

"Right." Will stood up to make an announcement. "Tonight Paige is in the dust, no offence Daaisi. The message said it's 'party time'. Daaisi can you please play Beastie Boys, Fight for your right, up loud for me."

Eugene smiled, he didn't know if Daaisi would take commands from others but on cue the guitar roared into life as the song filled the room. Will got up on the chair and started to gyrate in time.

"Where are the hot clubs in this sleepy den. This is a port town they have to be WILD!"

Eugene really didn't know, but was kind of caught by Will's enthusiasm. The two had been great friends and done a lot together as kids, at Uni and as adults. Crazy things. The two of them kind of set each other off.

"Here!" Will shouted over the music "Lets go to Club Blu it looks pretty close. We can Uber it."

"Daaisi can you get us an Uber to Club Blu?" Will shouted over Mike D, MCA and Ad-Rock.

The music turned down slightly as Daaisi's voice blended in "Uber will arrive in seven minutes."

"Yeah. You gotta fight for your right to paaarrrttyy!" Will belted out the chorus revving up Eugene.

***

Wim looked at the Dream Bakery from across the street.

It was beautifully finished in a modern way. A way that also paid homage to the history of the building. He had checked out the market research company online and found nothing of substance. Before he visited he also checked out the history of the building and noticed it was purchased about three years ago for a steal and renovated at great expense. The company that had completed it seemed to be squeaky clean, taxes paid, everything perfect. The work was done under the banner of market research for financial companies, all of who seemed to be legitimate in the US, UK, across the EU and in Asia.

'Rare for modern companies to do that unless they are forced to,' he thought 'normally they would tear it down and replace it with glass and steel'.

Wim rang the bell, but got no answer so he knocked on the glass door, still with no answer. It was hard to tell from the outside if anyone was inside. The windows were mirrored and there were no lights or sounds from anywhere.

He put his card in the door and turned to leave, he walked about ten steps and heard someone walk up behind him and push the same button and say "Daaisi, let me in."

Wim turned and retraced his steps quickly, just catching the door before it closed. The man who entered was quick to turn and face Wim before he got inside.

"Hey there, no piggybacks." he said with his hands up.

Wim held up his badge and stooped to pick up his card that had fallen out of the door, handing it over. The man was a medium height, with a medium build, he had brown hair and hazel eyes. Wim thought he was in his forties and in those few words he had already picked out the Australian accent.

"I am looking for whoever is in charge to discuss a participant in your research. His name was Lem Forth. Do you have some time now?"

"Mate," he said, using the term in the Australian way, not alluding to friendship but just as a disarming term for someone who's name you don't know, can't remember or choose not to use. "That would be Genie but he hasn't come in yet, we had a big night. Haven't seen him for years, you know."

"So you don't work here?" Wim asked with a serious tone.

"Nope," he said as he looked at the floor. It gave Wim the feeling that this man was out of place.

"What about Daisy? Does she work here?" Wim had caught the name as he walked off.

"Automated house, has vocal recognition. State of the Art." the man said proudly.

"Right." Wim had heard of such technology but had never encountered it.

"So you are the only two people currently using this premises?" Wim pressed.

"Yep," he added "and I don't know Genie's business one little bit."

"OK," Wim wasn't getting anywhere. "Do you mind to give my card to Genie? I will call again tomorrow if I don't hear from him."

"I'm sure he will call." the man said with a smile, not forced, more the smile of someone who had confidence in the way things would go. Wim knew that smile, he had seen it on a hundred questionable people and noted in his book he would need to follow up on what goes on here, before moving himself outside.

***

Will grabbed a large bottle of still water and moved into the second interview room which he had made his home. He immediately called Eugene who didn't answer so Will left a him a cryptic voicemail

"Mate, jack minus the divvy just came and went, snooping like blue, you need to get your arse back pronto."

Will was jumpy, he had been coming down from some very nice ecstasy followed by a few ecstatic hours with a particularly tall blonde named Famke, before his encounter with Wim. Where was Eugene?

"Daaisi is Eugene here?" he said out loud.

"No Will," Daaisi's voice bled into the room confidently.

"Do you have GPS coordinates on Eugene?" he said, hoping.

"Yes Will, but I am not at liberty to divulge those to you." Daaisi replied seeming to add an almost authoritarian tone.

"Right, but, is he close by? Say five hundred meters or less." Will was hoping to work this a bit. He always thought no was such a final word.

"No Will. Eugene is asleep which would explain why your call would not connect."

"Right-o," Will was getting somewhere. "Has he been asleep for long?" The two had got separated after Will had hooked up with Famke, looks like Eugene had also found some refuge.

"No Will."

"OK, can you let me know when he gets home, like wake me up if I'm asleep." Will was almost pleading with Daaisi.

"Yes Will," Daaisi responded confidently.

Will settled on the day bed and closed his eyes. He would normally think that was a close call but it didn't appear they were looking for him or even knew who he was, so that was all on Eugene.

What has he been up to, Will wondered?

Dark Horse.

***

Wim returned to the station.

He had a bad feeling about that Bakery but nothing conclusive. He could pass this case off as Aunt died, nephew who was reliant on her lost it and died from a heart attack on a cold night, not really prepared for the weather change. Seven people died that night from exposure in Rotterdam. But unlike this case, not one of them was five hundred meters from their apartment with keys in their pockets and not one of them had five hundred Euros in their wallet.

The Coroner had not performed any inspection or autopsy yet so he would need to wait on that.

Lem seemed to have no friends, no contacts, no enemies, there was no sign of struggle and no weapon. Apart from the Dream Bakery, he had no enquiries to follow up on.

Wim had six other cases he needed to follow up on so couldn't give this one much more time.

***

Eugene didn't need to open his eyes to know he was not where he should have been.

He was naked and his head felt very dusty.

Dusty not in a, drank too much way, more in a 'what did I take again' way. He was thirsty and in contradiction he needed to urinate. Eugene moved slightly and his arm brushed up against something warm.

Someone warm.

A few of the nights escapades came back to him but as his senses returned he struggled to remember her name.

Eugene slid softly off the bed and made his way to the en-suite bathroom. The place looked vaguely familiar but he needed get his urgent business out of the way before he focused on anything further afield. After a surprisingly very short trip to the bathroom he finally came out of the fog and recognised the Hilton. He had stayed here a lot when he first came to work for Shell, the main Shell office was walking distance.

'I must have been on autopilot,' he thought.

'Hana,' his memory came back in a flood. 'Right. Club Blu.'

He went back towards the bed and collected his clothes and hers, they were discarded randomly but he put them in separate piles, hers close to the bed and his on the chair at the desk except his Tommy Hilfiger stretch boxer shorts which he put on.

Returning to the bathroom Eugene ordered some room service using the bathroom phone. Coffee and danish.

Simple.

Eugene went back to the bedroom but Hana was still asleep. He looked again, she looked very cute in a Japanese way, like a manga character. Maybe it was the way her purple streaked black hair fanned out against the Hilton's white striped sheets.

He sat down at the desk and checked his phone.

A call from Will and a voicemail. Some security footage from Daaisi, looks like someone caught Will at the door, great. He didn't really want to get to that business now, seemed a bit disingenuous with Hana still asleep.

On cue, she rustled slightly.

Eugene quickly moved to the bed and slid under the covers. She turned and put her arm over his body, opened her eyes and smiled. Wow, what a beautiful smile Eugene thought. Whatever else they had discussed or done or taken last night it was that smile that got him here. That and maybe an Uber.

"Hi." Hana said in a dreamy voice.

"*Ohayō*" Eugene said.

"Oh, you're so lovely," she giggled.

Eugene had stayed for about six months in this particular Hilton and a lot in the many other Hilton's dotted through out the world. When he ordered room service, things happened quickly, even though he didn't ask for it. So it was super speedy to get the simple order of coffee and Danish and it arrived at that moment.

Hana looked up at him nervously as the door bell rang.

"I ordered some coffee for us" he smiled grabbing the robe from the cupboard and heading for the door.

He returned with a well adorned breakfast trolley and the room warmed with the smell of fresh coffee and pastries.

"Oh wow." Hana exclaimed. "All that before I get my head off the pillow. You were not kidding when you said you were a guy that gets things done."

Eugene smiled. "Did I say that?"

"I don't usually drink coffee," Hana smiled, "but that smells wonderful."

"They do a great filter coffee here." Eugene replied. "I am more of an espresso machine guy myself but this will do the trick."

The two settled in around the coffee and enjoyed a brief moment together.

Eugene looked on Hana's face and into her eyes and saw a beautiful soul. Full of energy and life but somewhat peaceful at the same time.

"Do you live here in Rotterdam?" She asked, "you are not Dutch."

"Yes. I live here. I am lucky, my father was German so I can live in Europe, my mother was British so I can come and go in the UK and I was born in Australia." Eugene felt very fortunate for the mix of nationalities that made up his heritage.

"Oh," Hana grinned. "Koala bear is my favourite."

Eugene laughed.

Finishing her coffee Hana grabbed him around the waist and removed his robe and Tommy Hilfiger's to show just how much she liked that Koala bear.

For Eugene everything else just had to wait.

Chapter Four

One step at a time

Paige was brutally startled awake, again. She hated that jolting feeling you got when the dream released you back into consciousness, like the turning point of a showground ride. To make matters worse Charlotte was still sound asleep next to her despite Paige's twitching. How do some people get the 'sleep through a bomb going off next to me' gene and some don't?

Paige's sleep after sex was usually the best, she was even known to snore heartily after an orgasm or two. These last few weeks had just been these edgy realistic dreams, not so much of terror, but of trepidation and full of jump scares without a payload.

She wasn't so sure, but maybe it was Charlotte.

Paige had always had a leaning both ways. She found girls very attractive, especially mousy blonde girls like Charlotte. She had a few casual affairs but this was her first try at some sort of a relationship and she was getting a bad vibe, it was all just a little bit too girly for her. There was no way she was taking on the manly role and overall without it she felt like something was missing.

Her dreams weren't helping. When you feel apprehensive and tense all night, its hard to just shake it off in the morning. It really didn't matter how good the coffee was, and Charlotte made really good coffee.

"Sorry babe," Charlotte said groggily sitting upright. "Did I sleep through again?"

"No" Paige said stolidly.

"Right," Charlotte fell back onto her over sized pillow and closed her eyes.

Paige waited just a minute or two, just to see what Charlotte would do. It's never a good sign when you are waiting out your partner.

Paige had met Charlotte through her work friend Emma. Charlotte worked selling roasted coffee beans into coffee shops, she used to be a Barista but took the upgraded pay scale into sales with a bonus of less time on her feet. Paige had been doing marketing for the overarching corporation that owned the coffee distribution network, among other things, and was on very good terms with Emma who was the sales manager. Charlotte and Paige met while out for Emma's birthday, it was a good night and both ended up hooking up with guys that knew each other. As chance should have it they saw each other a few times after and ended up swapping numbers and chatting a bit more. Not sure why, but when Charlotte's thing ended with her guy she turned to Paige for some company. Nothing sordid, just a few drinks and a chat. Paige was doing her on again off again dance with the guy she met at the party and just as that was coming to a conclusion Charlotte kissed her, and she liked it.

Paige was never one to announce a relationship, but her friends could see something was going on and it didn't take them long to figure out the new girl, Charlotte, was touching the right buttons for Paige. The casual physical turned regular and when Charlotte had the apartment she rented purchased from under her, she moved in with Paige. It was suppose to be temporary but it had been a month now. Paige felt a little powerless and that is just not where she wanted to be. Maybe that's where the dreams were coming from, that powerless feeling was what she had with Eugene, and these dreams were the same. The boy, the warnings, the urgent highly emotive, compelling cautions, remonstrated repeatedly. 'Get Out'.

She lay there, naked under the duvet, waiting, thinking. Life in conscious time somehow didn't grab her as completely as time did in dreams.

Paige had to be careful, she didn't want to hurt Charlotte and she did love having her around.

"I'm on it." Charlotte slipped out the side leaving Paige intact in the warmth. Her slim very white skin a beautiful foil for Paige's erratically tanned asian tone.

'Finally,' Paige thought.

Now that her dream anxiety had subsided Paige ran through last night in her mind. The castle, the excessively melted candles, the stark walls illuminated by cascading lightning strikes, so close but without the accompanying rumble of thunder, the parapets, the walls crumbling as the rain beat against them. all of that merge and twisting finally disappearing into a kaleidoscope of purple fractals

Paige looked at her reflection in her mobile phone. She flattened her hair a little and looked again teasing a few strands loose at the front to make her hair look like it had fallen effortlessly into a cascade of cuteness.

Moments later Charlotte returned with two perfectly constructed latte's.

"Babe, you look so beautiful in the morning. I could just eat you up, again."

"I could be eaten." Paige smiled, "but life says, work must come first and I get to come later."

Charlotte grinned openly, the cat that knew the cream was still to come.

Paige let herself be momentarily encapsulated by the coffee, the aroma, the beautiful art on top, a swan riding on a love heart. She took a low draft to let the nutty taste wash around in her mouth before letting it run down her throat. The silky liquid supercharged her senses instantly.

"What's your plan today?" Paige asked.

"Well I have a day off, thought I might look for a place. Like, I really appreciate you letting me stay and some days I am just in heaven but I know you like your space and if this is going to work I think it might be better if we take it a little bit at a time."

Paige looked at Charlotte with her best sad face, she deployed it with just enough real life concern and a smidgen of 'it's for the best'.

"No hurry," Paige smiled "you find something that suits you."

"Thanks Babe." Charlotte leaned down and kissed Paige deeply. The nutty taste of the coffee masking the nights effect on her breath.

Paige rolled Charlotte over in the bed and the two embraced tightly. Charlotte's hands slipped down over Paige's hips but Paige had no time.

"I gotta go Angel." Paige raised her eyebrows towards the huge clock on the wall.

Charlotte held Paige's fingertips until the two separated, both holding the pose for a few seconds in a fleeting attempt to replicate the Sistine Chapel's breath of life providing an awkward moment. Paige giggled and moved toward the en-suite bathroom to take a shower.

Once upon a time a shower was a mystical wonderland, a place where Paige could let her day dreams wander in and out of the whimsy of her imagination. She could pick the flowers, smell them, re plant them and watch the unicorns eat them. But this life, this truly adult life, made no allowances for such frivolity. The waiting for the warm water was tortuous so she busied herself ordering the various bottles of shampoo, face cleanser, conditioner and body scrub. Charlotte had moved in her set of bottles next to Paige's and there just wasn't room on the tiny shelf embedded into the wall. Paige had noticed early that Charlotte didn't throw away the empty bottles and just left multiples of bottles both full and empty sitting there. She would also often leave one centimetre left in a bottle, so this had become how Paige passed the time, waiting for the water to warm up.

The mechanical act of cleanliness transpired in an instant, once the conditions were right. The effects of the coffee took over, and the water gave her mind further lucidity. The savagery of the day dawned and pierced Paige in multiple places simultaneously. Her head felt like it had been cleaved, just holding on by the hair around her scalp, but worse, her heart ached.

This morning had been a good start but a change was needed and she resolved within herself not to make it harsh. Paige still felt bad about the way she had treated Eugene, less so about the way she had treated everyone else since Eugene, but wanted to think karma needed her to lift her game.

Mostly dry and more ready to face the world Paige moved back to the bedroom to find Charlotte had gone. Dressing quickly and then redressing into something more appropriate Paige noticed a message on her phone.

"At the gym..."

"Damn!" Paige cursed.

"Eight thirty Seven a.m."

She was going to be late. Even if the tube was on time, which it never was, she was twenty minutes plus from work.

Paige skipped the breakfast that she never ate again, grabbed her keys and her coat and urged her body out the door. She wasn't tired or sore, the events of the previous night were probably more uplifting than not, but without a doubt her soul was damaged and that made her feel continuously deflated.

The outside waiting to embrace her was very dead London. A sky that wanted to cry in its sadness but couldn't find the energy. Air that formed a mist to shroud the daily dreariness of the two up two down buildings that lined the street. Streets of houses trying so hard to be homes but instead showing their lack of soul like a throbbing raw wound.

'Once upon a time, someone had a plan that looked orderly and neat and beautiful' she thought, 'and then people had to screw it up by imprinting their realities all over that perfect design.'

Paige chastised herself, as she had no time for the architecture. The Angel tube station had its usually depraved cross section of humanity milling around. She bypassed them in haste with barely a judgement bestowed on even the shiftiest looking of the group.

Paige flashed a glance at the timing boards.

'All lies', she thought and emphatically pushed through the security gates to the platform.

The tube was surprisingly on time and even more surprisingly not a damned vessel of human sardines. She didn't get a seat but her expectations were met as the tube delivered her to Bank station in nineteen minutes.

She was late but not that late, so all would be forgiven.

She burst through the doors to the office and, as was her routine, headed straight for the tearoom. The office was quiet.

A little too quiet.

Paige checked her smart watch to make sure it was a work day and she hadn't got it wrong.

She promised herself she wouldn't do that again.

No, it was a proper day.

A routine is a routine and hers was straight to the tea room so she hustled down the corridor and turned quickly into the small break out room at the end.

She was very surprised to see a long line of extremely glum faces. All in the tea room.

"Good Morning All," she tried so hard to put on her best happy but not too happy face. They were all at work after all. You save the truly happy face for a party or the pub or somewhere else.

"Not so, I'm afraid," said Grace.

Paige looked around the room waiting for someone to fill her in. Company bankruptcy, industry shakeup, ransomware. What was it. She looked around pleadingly but no-one was giving anything away.

"It's Charles," Edith followed up. Edith was in accounts so she mouthed the words lacking empathy as was her way. Like Charles had just nipped out for the day.

"He's passed, last night," Bill followed up. Bill was usually very bouncy and full of fun.

"In his sleep."

"Oh," Paige slipped out.

Not in an "Oh" like the puzzle had been solved and she had the answer, even though that's sort of how she felt. Also not an "Oh" like she had just be pricked by a needle. More like an "Oh" as in oh dear. In this case a particularly small Oh as she really didn't have a great deal of respect or admiration or like of Charles, even if he was the boss.

"The other directors just left," Bill said in a bubbly way, like it was a bonus "They want business as usual, all hands on deck and so on."

"But we are thinking we might head home and have a few days of bereavement leave," piped in Aldrin who was among other things, the shop floor union representative.

"OK" said Paige in a mild attempt to support whatever was happening. She wasn't about to support days off without pay, not for Charles. But if the union was in for a few days paid, she wouldn't say no.

"So was it a heart attack," Paige chipped in. Everyone in the room looked around accusingly. Not directly at her but like she had said the thing that no-one needed to say.

"Indeed," said Harold. Harold was very used to stating the obvious as he was in middle management.

"You could almost see it coming," Paige let out. "He did play the game at both ends, always on the hunt day and night." While the conversation had been going on Paige had made herself a cup of tea so was now keen to exit. The tea room was her sanctuary from other people, she knew others used it but she always tried to avoid the times other people were in it. She wasn't keen to share it quite in this way.

"Was he alone?" she dropped as she walked out the door.

Paige had a feeling he wasn't. Possibly that girl from the Turner account or possibly the other one he kept on about or maybe another late night conquest. He was a manic Tinder user and spent most of his evening in pubs 'chatting up birds' as he liked to say. Not in an ornithological way.

At about that time Paige remembered the second section of her dream from that night. That was Charles having sex with another woman in the corner of her dream. No wonder she had blocked that out. Having the memory of it now was making her feel quite ill. But in the dream he had collapsed while he was in the middle of it and turned into a horse. A large black stallion with large chunks of decaying flesh hanging and glowing red eyes.

Back at her desk Paige set her workstation up with her email positioned carefully so she could concentrate on it for a while whilst looking like she was reviewing some extremely important documents on her workstation.

An email arrived from the other directors mourning Charles' passing and saying some quite nice words about him. Given none of the other directors liked him very much it did show how important he was to the company. They would miss him was more a statement that they now had to do his work and the fact was none of them were anywhere near as good at it as he was. Whatever his gross habits were from a human stand point, Charles was a very good business operator. He was good with customers, good with contracts, good with giving people what they wanted whilst keeping a sizeable chunk money in the exchange for himself or his company.

The dream came flooding back to Paige in more detail. Charles was actually in it before she saw him in the act, he was talking some nonsense to her. Something about being in the wrong place and needing to get back to the place you know you need to be.

Paige took a long breath over the lip of her teacup before sipping a delicious mouthful.

She turned to Grace on the desk next to her and asked. "What time did he go? Charles."

Grace looked at her with a strange macabre look. Like she didn't want to discuss it even though she knew the answer.

"Early this morning" she replied gingerly. "I think Gerald said it was one or two am."

Paige nodded her appreciation.

One am, pub closed at eleven, an hour to get whoever he was with home and hour on the job before whatever popped, popped.

She had woken up at two thirty a.m., the dream had been long and intricate as many of hers were, but the Charles bit was at the end.

'Something in that,' she mused.

Eugene would know. He had many theories but he was very sure that dreams crossed among other things, consciousnesses. Sleeping, waking, past, future, present, things seen and things experienced were all put into the mixer and regurgitated in a meaningful way, nightly. If you only knew what the meaning was or how to interpret the images.

"We're out," said Aldrin placing a letter in front of Paige stating that staff who worked under Charles were allowed two days emotional leave to grieve.

He moved on quickly to distribute more of his prize letters.

Paige didn't wait, leaving her steaming tea cup on her desk as she made for the exit.

***

Eugene pressed on the newly unlocked door. He had heard the click as he approached, he knew Daaisi watched for his arrival. The routine had played out hundreds of times since the Dream Bakery was finished. He walked in and lifted a bottle of Evian from the fridge. He opened it in the servery and downed the whole thing discarding the empty bottle into the recycle bin by the fridge.

"Thirsty Mate?" Will had also heard the click and had migrated from the interview room that had become his room, to the servery.

"Where did you get to?" Eugene responded drily.

"Same could be asked of you my good sir," Will retorted accusingly. "Was that the little Japanese kid," he added removing something from Eugene's collar.

Eugene couldn't help but produce a big smile.

"Only you could own a beautiful, state of the art, private pad like this and not bring a girl back here." Will had a huge grin which quickly changed.

"Did you see my messages?"

"I did," Eugene said calmly. "Piggy's with sticky beaks are a global infestation," he added.

"What did he want?"

"Just a chat," Will shrugged handing Eugene Wim's card.

"I'll call him a bit later," Eugene was in no hurry. "So how was your night around Rotterdam's closest nightspot?" Eugene quizzed Will.

"Well, I would say Wow!" Will grinned. "A man could learn to like having those big tall blond ladies around. They smile so sweet and seem so very lost in this Australian accent."

"I'm sure it's your stunning personality mate," Eugene retorted, knowing the jibe would be taken in good spirit.

"Can we go again?" Will looked at Eugene with big puppy dog eyes.

"Some more Grolshies might help me convince you."

"A reminder that subject 261 will be arriving at two pm for a previously scheduled appointment." Daaisi cut in.

"Party pooper." Will said turning on his heels and looking at the speaker in the roof that Daaisi came in from. "I might make myself scarce then."

Eugene smiled. He knew that Will's retreat would be temporary and that the two of them would likely have more words later on that afternoon.

He also knew he had to call the police officer and he needed to be sharp for that so he set a quick schedule, shower, coffee, police, appointment. He could deal with Will after all that.

Moving through his schedule quickly and now with his coffee in hand Eugene called the number on the card from his home based mobile phone. Eugene kept a number of devices for different purposes but this one rarely, if ever left the Dream Bakery.

"Wim Hummel," the gruff sound of the voice made it clear to Eugene that Wim was an old school detective.

"Hello, detective. This is Eugene Baltes you left a card at my address, the dream bakery, today. My friend wasn't sure what it was regarding but apparently you asked that I call as soon as possible."

"Yes, Mr Baltes, thank you for calling back so promptly."

"No problems, how can I assist you?" Eugene was on his best behaviour and very formal.

"I am making enquiries about the more recent movements of Mr Lem Forth." Wim's words were straight from the police speak handbook.

"Yes," Eugene replied quickly. "I think Lem is due here the day after tomorrow, let me check my appointment schedule." Eugene made some tapping noises on his keyboard while he was talking.

"Right," said Wim. "Exactly what is the appointment for? Your friend wasn't able to tell me."

"Yes, he has just arrived in from Australia, we were actually out last night all night catching up, like old times." Eugene felt the additional information wasn't needed but showed he was going about his business as usually. "Here at the dream bakery we do fintech market research. Much of which is covered by an NDA due to the sensitive market nature. Mr Forth is assisting with product research on a volunteer basis."

"OK," the detective said non-committally. He was letting Eugene do the talking but Eugene was just about done being the chatty one.

"Was there something else you wanted to know Detective? I have another appointment this afternoon which I need to prepare for. "

Wim took a breath. It wasn't the first time he had these conversations. "Do you know of any associates of Mr Forth or his movements in the last few days."

"Mr Forth is a volunteer here, we don't really mix in any social way. I know he said he has an Aunt. To be honest he seems a bit of a loner to me." Eugene was trying to be helpful but not too helpful. "He was here on Wednesday and as I said he is due back next Tuesday."

"Yes," Wim confirmed. "About that. I am calling because Mr Forth has been found deceased. It is routine that we follow up all known contacts even when there are no suspicious circumstances."

Those words were sweet music to Eugene's ears but he kept his composure. "Really, I am truly shocked to hear that. He seemed fine on Wednesday, a little spacey maybe, to be honest I wasn't sure but he seemed like he may have taken something recently, maybe only Cannabis but it seemed out of character. He has visited us a few times here and has been very helpful in our research. The week before last we actually got a car to pick him up and drop him off as he got lost on the way here."

"Really," Wim replied. "Anything else you noticed?"

Eugene was pretty sure he didn't want to give anything else away. That was enough to plant the seed, the rest would need germinate before he added anything else.

"Nothing comes to mind right now."

"OK," Wim replied. "Thank you for your information Mr Baltes. Please get in touch with me if you think of anything else."

"Of Course I will," Eugene kept his tone polite and helpful. "Have a good afternoon detective."

"You also," Wim replied ending the call quickly.

***

Ruud had grown up in Rotterdam.

A very promising football career had been destroyed at age thirteen by a series of anterior cruciate ligament injuries and subsequent reconstructions and subsequent failures. He could be called a living example of the failures of sports medical science. Thankfully, this is something that has improved greatly in the years since he stopped playing football, but all to no avail for Ruud.

So today Ruud was what he was, not in retaliation for the hand of cards he had been dealt, but more in reaction to the circumstances he found himself. If you leave a hungry man in a room with food its only a matter of time before his instincts insists he eats.

So after the contract at Feyenoord was gone he found a niche in the Rotterdam community at the old harbour. Many people would just label him a criminal but to Ruud he was a little more sophisticated than that.

He identified as a gender neutral confidence worker.

Others, particularly in the court system, had labelled him a swindler, shark, fraud and scammer. Like many in his line of work he had done some minor time in prison, just enough to learn a lot from those around him. They all shared the tricks of trade in the hope that the things they learned would stop them from being repeat offenders, this was especially true of those in the confidence game. Ruud had spent many hours behind bars learning from the best how to cajole, persuade, coax, seduce, lure and entice people into doing things they wouldn't do if they knew all the facts surrounding the interaction.

Some days Ruud would just relax and enjoy the fruits of his hard earn grift and thankfully today was one of those days. Yesterday he had been particularly lucky and made a big score. So today he was living large with a few drinks at the White House.

That was until Will walked into the bar.

Nothing else changed about Ruud, not the way his clothes fell or his physical demeanour, not his hair or his smile. Just his focus.

From what he could see outwardly, Will had recently come into some money or some luck. Most importantly, Will was looking to size-ably increase whatever he had in the shortest time possible. The experience Ruud had meant he could tell all that from the way Will walked from the door to the bar. He had already made a quick decision to try the straight up approach but was stopped in his tracks when Will opened his mouth and ordered a beer. Two things made him reconsider. First Will was Australian, second was that Will was himself in the game.

It is a truly refined art to recognise someone in your line of work just by the way they order a beer, such was the way of the Confidence Artiste. Ruud now needed to pivot slightly, not too much, but slightly. Now it was the long game.

Will stood tall and proud at the bar, he had positioned his body so that his focus was away from Ruud. He had clearly seen Ruud and Ruud had to assume, as they were of similar nature, he had already confirmed the same thing about Ruud, that he had about Will. So Ruud waited a little while, tempered his drink, let Will settle at the bar and then travelled the short distance to replenish his hard earned beer.

As he approached he let his right leg collapse.

"Damn," he swore.

"You right mate," Will had offered his arm but unable to stop the fall was now helping Ruud to his feet.

"Thanks, yeah, I'm good."

"Another beer Goos and one for my saviour here," he motioned to the bartender.

"Thanks mate but I can't accept a beer from a stranger." Will added.

"Ruud," Ruud said offering his hand to be shaken.

"Will," Will responded in kind as for an Australian it is very rude not to.

"Strangers no more, Goos." Ruud re-motioned to the bartender who had now stationed himself in the general area.

"Old war wound?" Will enquired.

"Repeated football injury," Ruud replied.

"He could have been one of the greats," Goos chimed in placing the newly poured beers on the bar.

Ruud raised his hands to silence the crowd.

"Long passed and truly forgotten."

Ruud told Will his story and the two of them shouted each other a few more beers. Ruud knew his angle here would not be a single transaction but a series of carefully planned steps. The first was confidence. Not trust, just confidence.

"So what do you do now," Will asked as part of the ongoing conversation.

"I do things around the port. I help to get things through where they perhaps might find it difficult. I suppose you might call me a shipping agent." Ruud laughed.

The afternoon went quickly and it was time for Will to head back to the Dream Bakery as per his promise to Eugene.

He exchanged numbers with Ruud and was gone.

Ruud settled back to enjoy the rest of his day. The Australian seemed a nice guy, but this changed his plan not one little bit.

***

Eugene was a little on edge, not in an all consuming way but everything small that he would usually let go became a big deal. The latest test subject was a giggly girl, slightly overweight and plain looking. She over compensated for her ordinary looks with an overly loud personality which was spearheaded by a particularly annoying laugh. It sent a shiver up Eugene's spine on first listen and got worse as the appointment progressed.

After the introductions he pretty much let Daaisi take care of the whole appointment to distance himself, but the echo of that laugh seemed to reverberate through the usually sterile halls of the Dream Bakery.

Truth is Eugene was preoccupied with the morning's conversation. Running it through in his mind to see if he slipped up in some way or if the police detective gave away that he picked up something untoward. He had Daaisi play back the conversation a few times and search everywhere possible to see if there was any movement on the case. There was nothing, but the silence wasn't soothing, actually the silence seemed to get louder as time went on.

The test subject finished the session and he made her coffee in silence. Well he was silent, mostly because she didn't shut up. Her incessant talking and all encompassing laughter made his mood worse and after presenting the coffee he excused himself and let Daaisi present the picture and direct the subject out the door.

Eugene headed back to his private quarters, showered and tried to remain calm and quiet. He felt there were a million things he could do but they were all peripheral. He knew if he continued to check on Lem's case he would either alert someone to his attempts or go mad in the process.

He could feel the relief when Will came home, not because Will would help but he knew the distraction would be the reward.

"Good one Mate?" Will questioned as Eugene entered the kitchen. Will had already opened a Grolsch and motioned to Eugene that he should join him.

Eugene held for a moment. He really didn't think alcohol would help.

"Yeah Na," Eugene replied. "Test subject was one of those over the top annoying personalities. Got right under my skin."

"Yeah, I hate that." Will nodded "So what did the cop say?" Will was always straight to the point.

Eugene changed his mind, opened the glass door of the display fridge and extracted an ice cold Grolsch. He popped the top with a refined skill that showed years of experience and took a refreshing mouthful. All this time, respecting the need and the tradition, Will waited patiently to have his question answered.

"Yeah, nothing to do with me," Eugene replied adding a small belch to give the statement the lightness he knew it needed to shake Will off the scent.

"Can't be nothing if they are hounding you," Will jibed.

"Just a test subject, who came here a few times, died. So this was a follow up. The guy didn't have a lot of friends, apparently, so the options were limited on who to ask. I told him all I could. Nothing much else to say."

"Right-o," Will didn't look convinced but had a few other things on his mind.

"How's was your afternoon?" Eugene added in quickly to move the subject on. "Catch any local sights?"

"Actually I went for a bit of a walk, ended up down at the old harbour." Will clearly had something he wanted to say, "met a few locals, had a few drinks and a few of those *Saucijzen Broodje*. Tasty little morsels they are."

"Nice," Eugene offered his beer in a drinkers salute which Will accepted, joining his beer to Eugene's. "Dutch street food is very meaty. I can take you to the Markthal later, best you'll get around here all in one place. The rest can be pretty spread out."

"Few more of these might be on the cards," Will added getting up to fetch two more. Eugene had barely absorbed half of his first drink so adopted the convention of swilling the remainder to catch up.

"That's the spirit," Will added in congratulations of Eugene's act.

"One of the guys I was drinking with had some work going, so I might follow him up on that." Will looked around the kitchen non-noncommittally.

"Sweet," Eugene enquired. "What sort of work?"

"Less you know the better I suppose." Will was again not making eye contact but after a pause squared his gaze on Eugene. "I might need a bit of seed funding, if you can help me out."

Now it made sense to Eugene.

"Seed funding?" Eugene replied "You know those plants are legal here and the game is pretty competitive."

"Nah, it's none of that. Just need a bit of capital for transport, tools and other stuff."

"Right," said Eugene. "What sort of money are we talking?"

"10,000 Euros ought to cover it. I reckon I could get it back to you in a month. Just need some buy in money."

Eugene looked at his friend. He wanted to help and figured it would come back to him in a month or later.

"Yeah OK."

"Thanks Mate."

Now it was Will's turn to bring things back around.

"So the guy that died was a test subject. What are you testing them for?"

"I told you, a few years ago I decided to pursue one of my pet projects. I have always had a fascination with dreams so I used some of my know how and some of my money to fund a way to equate brain patterns to images. At first I was just testing on myself but that caused some complications, so I moved that testing onto my ex, Paige, which caused even more complications. So, I cooked up this scheme to use students and the general community to let me test on them. The guy that died was test subject number 259. They get some bitcoin..." Eugene held his fingers up to his lips to signify it was all done without the knowledge of any relevant authorities. "and I get to the keep the test data. More recently I started giving the test subjects a single rendered still image which kind of sent the whole thing on a different trajectory."

"So you monitor dreams and present a photo?" Will seemed perplexed. "Why?"

"To be honest I was looking for some personal answers," Eugene looked introspectively around the room. "Ended up with more questions, which now I just need to follow through."

"Well it certainly made you a little bit famous," Will grinned. "I saw your name mentioned in the Philippines."

"The Dream Photographer," Will smiled and performed a sweeping gesture with his hands like he had just completed a magic trick. "I wondered where that moniker came from."

"Yeah," said Eugene.

"Not ideal but sometimes that stuff happens."

"Can I have a go?" Will pleaded.

"Not under the influence," Eugene said. "I had some issues early on with people on drugs or drink."

"I have another appointment tomorrow but after that I reckon we can squeeze you in. What do you think Daaisi?"

"The interview rooms both have sufficient threshold and general measurements to accommodate Will-I-used-to-be."

Will burst out laughing.

"Daaisi. That was a colloquial term for the ability to arrange an appointment. You should review that answer."

"Yes Eugene," Daaisi's voice seemed to take on a cold tone.

"Oops," Will smiled. "I think I upset her."

"Technically not a her, and I haven't written the code for upset, nor given the ability for emotional responses to be added. Baby steps."

The two friends laughed.

Chapter Five

Face Up

"I know pet," Adrie screeched in wild agreement. "Amazing."

She shifted onto the ball of her foot, like she was a kid again preparing to take an Arabesque pose in ballerina classes. She was still glowing with awe from her appointment a few days ago, unable to resist telling anyone and everyone who would listen.

"The girls and I had a long lunch yesterday at Mendoza and I showed it off," she smiled widely as she loved to be the centre of attention. "If you want to meet for coffee in the morning I can bring my iPad. I can't send it pet, there is this long legal NDA, no copies allowed in any form."

"Let's go to Kuub Coffee, down by Markthal. 10:30 pet, so don't be late."

Adrie was glowing, in her moment. Turning, she noticed a large dust patch that she had missed, maybe when Saskia called. She smiled again and returned to her cleaning.

She looked up from her task and saw Douglas move gingerly, he was trying hard to be deliberate as he came down the stairs. It was something that last week he would have taken for granted, but this week he needed to be sure, as a fall would surely be the end for him.

He didn't look up but focused on his movement placing each foot with great care, establishing himself on that step before attempting the next. As a result, he looked very old.

"You OK pet," Adrie's heart broke to see Douglas in this way.

"Yeah," he replied. "Just taking it slow. Can't imagine a fall would be good right now."

"No, a fall would not be good, now or anytime." Adrie used her most caring voice. "Please pet, take care of yourself."

Douglas nodded nonspecifically. He looked down at his slippers with a troubled gaze.

"Now. You know I have a repeat session with 'The Dream Photographer' tomorrow," she beamed proudly. "Are you going to be OK here on your own or should I get one of the girls to drop around?"

"I'll be fine," he groaned. "Maybe this time I will hang around down here instead of upstairs. Just for a change of scenery."

"Great idea!" Adrie exclaimed, "we will set you up with extra pillows and you can watch the big TV in home cinema mode. Maybe one of those extra long spaghetti westerns you love."

Adrie watched as Douglas shuffled over to the bookshelf where they kept the DVD's and extracted the directors cut of The Good, The Bad and The Ugly. She knew it was over four and a half hours. Someone had given it to him as a gift and to her knowledge he had never been able to find the time to watch it while staying awake. This may just be that moment. He held it up proudly like he had just caught a fish.

Adrie clapped and cheered. Things weren't so bad.

***

The plastic cover that held all the electronics in appeared to have a seam on the inside that rubbed away, almost autonomously, while she slept. It didn't feel uncomfortable when it was fitted or when she was conscious, but as soon as sleep engulfed her it seemed to perform minor twirls on the side of her head.

Adrie scratched at the cap meaninglessly. Her semi-conscious state unable to rectify the problem by removing the cap but equally unable to ignore its heightened irritation.

"The session has concluded and you may remove the dream interceptor at your leisure."

The building AI was very realistic, she pondered. She must remember to tell Douglas about that, he would be impressed. At first she thought it was a real person hidden away in another room, or another country. That accent was very much like Douglas's but perhaps with a hint that the person spoke a second language that was not European. Adrie had a good ear for that kind of thing.

She reached up gingerly and removed the cap and rubbed the part of her head that had made contact with the plastic seam.

Sitting up, she bought the room into focus. "Now for one of those fluffy latte's," she smiled. She did like the way this man made coffee. He was a bit aloof and quite mysterious in other ways but that skill grounded him as a man that appreciated the finer things in life.

"Please make your way into the kitchen when you are ready."

The accent was definitely London, English.

Early on Adrie had decided that she best not converse with the AI. Something in her just didn't see the point. She would happily interact on a functional level but there seemed little reason for conversation. Adrie loved a good conversation, but it had to be two ways, she needed to know the person she was talking with was engaged and enjoying the moment, she just couldn't believe that was going to happen with AI.

She went to rise from the daybed and felt a little woozy so dropped back down into the sitting position. Her vision blurred slightly but returned quickly. She remained still and took a few deep breaths. Feeling much better she attempted to rise again and this time successfully began the journey to the kitchen. She was greeted by Eugene, who was sitting at the table. He seemed to be most comfortable in his position behind the coffee machine and looked slightly cramped with his legs pushed together underneath and his hands folded on the surface.

"That hat has a seam that you can't even feel when you first slip it on, but seems to irritate my ear wildly while I am asleep." Adrie declared.

Eugene's expression didn't change. "Let me have a look at it."

"Thanks Pet."

"Everything else OK?" he queried.

"Yes," Adrie replied with a big smile. "Bit woozy waking up, must have been a good sleep."

"Yes," he replied. "My data shows you spent a good deal of time in slow-wave sleep, often hard to wake up from. Do you have any recollection from any dreams?"

"Sketchy at the moment," Adrie was definitely finding it difficult to wake up. "Might be better after one of those delicious latte's" she hinted with the subtlety of a small dentists drill.

"Of course."

Adrie sat opposite the seat that Eugene had occupied and looked at the chair he had vacated. She did not feel very awake at all. Her thoughts turned to the dreams she just had, but nothing came through, she just couldn't focus on what was going on. Unlike other times when the recollections were patchy, at this time there was nothing.

"Is it possible I didn't dream at all," she asked Eugene, who had busied himself collecting cups and jugs and other things he needed to complete his task.

"It is," he replied with a sense of knowing. "But, I was watching some of your read outs and I see a significant REM sleep period and some pretty high levels of brain activity which we would always account to dreaming."

"Ah OK," she smiled. "You know it pet. That's why you get the name."

Eugene smiled. It looked to Adrie a reasonably cheap fake smile. She supposed he didn't particularly like the name. Once he was sure Adrie wasn't going to continue talking he started the coffee grinder. The shrill tone filled the room with an all encompassing menace. Once the grind was complete the noise was replaced by the warm smell of fresh ground coffee and they both took a private moment to enjoy the aroma.

Adrie broke the silence to follow up her earlier query. "So why can't I remember even one detail of that dream, even though it was just right now?"

"These are things we are unsure of, it's part of my research. Better understanding of the process and hopefully through that understanding we can gain some insight or control."

"Control sounds a long way away," Adrie said flippantly.

"It may well be," Eugene replied. "But in my short time researching this I have made significant discoveries that go well beyond the photograph and the name."

"OK," Adrie replied, she was feeling so very poorly that she decided not to engage him further in the hope he would get on with the coffee, expediting her salvation.

Eugene had busied himself and after pouring two cups he moved to lengthen the milk.

"Won't be long," he said, his smiled seemed to change to the genuine article.

Adrie closed her eyes. Not because she was tired but to minimise the necessity to maintain her focus. It seemed all off.

"The picture shouldn't be long." Eugene said placing the cup in front of Adrie and retaking his seat opposite at the table. He breathed in heavily over his coffee enjoying the bouquet before sipping a small taste.

Adrie wasn't going to be so refined and quickly bought the cup to her lips to guzzle half of the contents.

"Oh you do make a nice coffee." She looked up to greet Eugene's kind intelligent green eyes. She held his gaze for a moment before returning to finish the coffee in a singular motion. Eugene smiled and sipped his brew slowly enjoying the experience. Daaisi broke the silence to advise the initial render would be ready in five minutes.

Adrie felt tired. Not quite ready to go just yet, although the walk home would probably do her good. No doubt the dull blue day had turned into an indigo afternoon accompanied in its song by an icy wind.

Eugene was sitting drinking his coffee peacefully. She had judged him last time as the quiet intelligent type. Not one to be engaged in gossip or idle chatter, so in her way she had kept quiet to see what the process and the results were. Now she had returned and she knew the results were worth the awkward nature of being here, being a test subject. So she matched his silence and patience waiting for the announcement that the render was complete.

Eugene rose and retrieved her cup and his. He moved silently to the kitchen and placed the dirty dishes in a drawer which looked like all the other drawers but was clearly a dishwasher. He obviously knew the process better than her but perhaps also had a better sense of time as in the completion of his cleaning up routine the AI cut in to advise the render was complete.

"Kitchen Monitor." He said impassively not supplying a target or any gratuity.

The render was of a bedroom. At first it looked like a hotel room but on closer inspection it was probably an apartment. There were various items scattered around that made it appear lived in. Some of the items looked familiar in some way. There was a man on the bed, a naked man. He was perched over an equally naked lady. From this vantage point the picture showed his back and his body as covering her upper body including her face. That back she knew, that was Douglas.

The other person she did not know, but she did know it wasn't her.

"Awkward," she said out loud.

"Not at all," Eugene said gently putting her at ease. "A recent study in Canada found that subjects of a sexual nature make up somewhere between five percent and ten percent of our dreams. I think the figure was precisely set at eight percent but I would say it is difficult to quantify without a very, very wide study."

"Well that's good to know," Adrie replied. She was a little mortified.

"Do you recognise anything?" Eugene asked in his methodical way.

"No, not from first glance," Adrie lied.

"Does this resemble the dream you have outlined before, the recurring dream. I think before you said it was erotic."

"Yes and No," Adrie wasn't sure what to say. She may have dreamed of the other woman before and in her regular dream there was a man, but she had never realised it was Douglas.

"How are you feeling?" Eugene enquired mostly to change the subject as he could see this was making Adrie feel uncomfortable. "Is that coffee kicking in OK?"

"Yes, yes, great. Thanks pet. I really should be going, I have things to get before the market closes."

"OK. No problems Adrie," Eugene said like he had a few things to do himself. "Can we reschedule another appointment next week? If you like we can put together a seed package which will uncover more detail on this dream or we can return to my standard seed package set and see where that takes us."

"Yes." Adrie's thoughts raced and with a flush of embarrassment. "Let's see more on this. If it's OK." she asked.

Eugene nodded. "Daaisi will be in touch to confirm the time but I will expect you at the same time next week. The high definition render will come as a link in an email tomorrow once it's complete."

"Great." Adrie replied, a moment of dread passed her thoughts, trying to think of a story she could tell her friends about why there was no picture. "I will see you then."

She quickly made her way out of the kitchen and headed for the servery to the exit and the future.

***

Will felt the visual of the explosion wash over him. A wall of sound rammed his auditory senses making him tilt back slightly on the day bed.

The movie was almost done. It had been the usual fast paced, thrill ride, good versus evil, special effects driven spectacular he liked to watch. Eugene had the best home cinema setup he had encountered which added a special gravitas to the bump and grind of the big budget action movie.

He received a message on his mobile phone from Eugene.

'My test subject has gone if you want to try.'

Will opened the door to his interview room and moved down the hall to the kitchen where he knew he would find Eugene.

"I've been stone cold sober all morning," he jibed. "Gotta be the first time in a decade or so."

Eugene laughed, "let's do it."

They went into the other interview room which was laid out neatly with the dream interceptor in place on the daybed.

"Daaisi has loaded the standard seed program. It's pictures and sounds of the seaside, intended to lead your dreams to provide a seaside location photograph. You watch them and listen as you are falling asleep and they influence the dream and provide your brain print of those objects and items to allow a picture to be rendered later. Nothing sinister, I promise."

"Right-o," Will almost looked enthusiastic. "Sleep perchance to ... and all that."

"You were just waiting for that moment, weren't you." Eugene smiled and slipped the dream interceptor over Will's head and shuffled it to fit. "Feel OK."

"Yep." Will let out a big yawn.

"Always in character," Eugene patted Will on the shoulder and made for the exit.

Will lay back on the bed.

"If you need to end the session for any reason just say 'terminate' and the session will cease," Daaisi came over the rooms speakers smoothly.

"You're in charge sweetheart." Will said as he lay back and waited for the images to wash over him.

***

In a dusty haze Will woke gently, flickering his eyes to adjust to the low light.

"That was painless," he quipped, possibly to Daaisi or even more possibly to no-one in particular.

He took his time to move to a sitting position before standing to stretch.

"Is Eugene around?" this time aiming the question squarely at Daaisi.

"Eugene is in the kitchen area waiting, monitoring your progress."

"Smells like beer o'clock then," Will grinned.

Daaisi processed the comment, breaking it into subject, predicate and object.

Beer did have a smell but the time reference made no immediate sense with either the ability or reaction to a smell, nor to the smell of beer. As per the predetermined final line of programming Daaisi chose to keep silent in response and as Will moved quickly out of the room it seemed an appropriate action.

"What a blast," Will joked as he entered the kitchen. "Didn't kill me so I must be stronger."

"It's a fairly innocuous procedure but I have my doubts about its long term affect. I noticed on myself and on most people who experience this procedure, that any more than five sessions can have an acute effect on the ability to distinguish dreams from reality."

"Say what?" Will almost choked on the beer he had extracted from the fridge. He slid the other one he was holding over the table to Eugene as the two of them locked eyes.

"Are you serious?"

Eugene gestured for Will to take a seat. "In my early experiments on myself, I was rudely interrupted in my dreams by this obstacle." Eugene displayed a render of the pink tiger striped snake on the screen. "It would appear when I was trying to seed and extract data from my dreams, at first surreptitiously blocking my view but then outwardly taunting me." Eugene cycled through his fifteen or so renders of the pink snake to show Will.

"Towards the later part of my self experimentation the affect on my mental state was noticeable and profound and eventually lead me to cease self experimentation completely."

This revelation had Will in a very quiet state which rarely occurred, so Eugene continued. About this time I met Paige who volunteered to take up the torch until the same snake and the same mental exhaustion overcame her, leading to her exit. She lasted a little bit longer than I did, but I also cared for her through the process and at the time I had an earlier version of Daaisi which only helped with data analysis and the trigger process."

"So how many sessions did the guy that died recently have?" Will asked, without knowing the spot he hit so very quickly.

"Subject 259 attended eight sessions," Daaisi cut in over the kitchens speaker system.

"So you still figure it wasn't you," Will shrugged. "But clearly you are onto something here."

"I think I am onto something, just not sure what demons I am fighting, personal or otherwise. Thus the test subjects, students etc."

"and now me," Will grinned.

"Yes mate, at your behest," Eugene reminded Will.

"Well, to be honest, it might have been better if we had this conversation prior to the session." Will said, feeling a little defensive.

It was Eugene's turn to smile "... and let you cop out and miss all the fun, no chance. The low level render is ready, you want to see?" Eugene put his hands in front of his eyes to mock Will who considering himself unmockable got up to retrieve another two beers from the fridge.

"Let's see it," he declared confidently.

The image was of the beach. Pretty much the same beach most people who undertake the initial image and sound seeded session dream. But the beach was empty, the sky a boring grey and the landscape barren.

"That's pretty boring mate," Will gesticulated. "Where am I?"

Eugene had been pondering some data on his laptop and looked up, pointing to a small spec on the horizon.

"Zoom in on the upper left quadrant third Zone right, seventh zone down. On the horizon."

Will figured the instructions were for Daaisi and had adapted quickly to the fact that there was a third person in every room waiting on every command responding without question.

"There you are, on a boat, headed out of town."

The two laughed.

"Yeah that'll be me," Will chimed in over Eugene's laughter.

"So let me get this straight, the pictures, the whale noises, lapping waves, seashells etc. etc. Show you how my brain processes images and from that when I reach a dream state you record the brain waves and compare them to come up with a collage of thoughts."

"In a nutshell. You did simplify the process rather a lot but that does seem to help people get a better grasp quicker, so lets go with that."

"So how did that boat get in there?"

"Did you dream of a boat?" Eugene asked.

"As a matter of fact I did," Will defended his question. "But how did you know that when there was no boat in the original seed pictures?"

"Daaisi is an extremely complex generative AI that can call on an enormous range of sources to best fit things known to your image. The decision engine looks at brain patterns matching the data we learn from you with the data we have on others and can bridge the gap. Dreaming about boats is not uncommon so I am going to guess the brain pattern was extracted from another test subject. Daaisi can you confirm this?"

"Seven percent of previous test subjects had dreams that included nautical themes, three percent with boats very similar to that you dreamed. Of that three percent there was a fifty percent pattern match on other objects in the standard dream seed package allowing me to make a simple match to your dream."

Will's jaw had dropped. "That is quite amazing. You are one clever cookie my friend."

Eugene continued, "Daaisi can extract data from a range of other sources, governments, corporations, archives not all of them Kosher, but all of them useful."

"Wow," Will lowered the tone "Whatever it takes eh."

Eugene's smile dropped a little, "Seemed inappropriate for them to hold onto that info."

"So what's the end goal," Will was truly fascinated and not being facetious.

"This is a voyage of discovery," Eugene pumped a fist into the air. "To boldly go.."

Will smiled. "No Idea huh?"

"None. I just wanted some answers, that just intensified after the whole thing with Paige."

"I think we have heard enough about Paige," Will said blankly. "Maybe we need another trip to Club Blu to see if that little Japanese girl isn't still hanging around."

"She headed back to Japan the next day," Eugene added impassively.

"Not what I meant, ya nong."

Will again made the walk to the fridge and extracted another two ice cold Grolsch. "Can't get AI to do that can we," he said dropping them on the table.

Eugene smiled, "I am of the belief that some tasks should be kept very human."

Chapter Six

Exposure

Wim had come to hate weekends.

Obviously not all weekends, just the ones he was enjoying and then had that enjoyment unceremoniously interrupted. Over the years it had built up in him a feeling of trepidation, almost a weekend phobia. They felt generally less satisfying as this apprehension clouded his potential relaxation.

So on Mondays when Wim returned to work to fulfil the nine to five part of his employment he often felt lethargic. This Monday was really no different than the last. Wim had a number of cases that were in a wide variety of states. His desk was piled with paper. An eclectic collection of police reports, coroner reports, information sheets, technical papers, newspapers and somewhere in there, his case files.

Monday's were Wim's day to piece together the puzzle of where everything belonged. Sometimes he could spend a significant part of the day just deciphering what report belonged where. As a case in point he read the report on the increase in knife usage in Charlois due to a high percentage of migrants from Northern Africa moving in on traditionally Eastern European territory.

Wim leaned back in his chair raising his coffee cup to his lips. He breathed shallowly and on getting a smell of the contents, changed his mind about drinking it. That report was for the Klarenden case. He didn't have so many cases he couldn't remember them, he saw that as his primary focus, keeping the detail of the cases under his care. He had noticed early on his career that missing information was the difference between a criminal that walked and a criminal that was convicted. He labelled them all guilty, it was his job to make sure there was evidence to make it stick.

He rectified the general order of two large folders and slid them into his credenza. The credenza was for open files, closed or cold went in the compactors to the left of the open plan office. If something made it there it was mostly out of his care or left to the future.

Wim shuffled a few other single page affidavits into a pile and distributed them into each individual case folder. Underneath he found some USB memory sticks containing CCTV footage. He checked the evidence stickers and found them all uploaded. So, collecting them into a group, he got up and moved them to the slot at the end of the room, which eventually ended up in the evidence room.

Now he was on his feet, Wim decided another coffee was in order.

Soon, with his fresh Coffee he returned to his desk. Top item was now a coroners report in the Forth case.

In big letters at the top it read 'Death by Exposure'.

Wim was not surprised. He scanned over the remainder of the report.

"Heart attack caused by environmental factors, no evidence of any external physical injury, some evidence of minor stroke in the posterior cingulate cortex, which is uncommon."

'Uncommon,' Wim pondered that word. That word wrapped up this case. The deceased had keys in his pocket and five hundred euros just five hundred meters from his apartment but died of exposure.

"Some evidence of recent cannabis use with trace elements of THC in the digestive system."

"OK," Wim said aloud, he might have an outcome. 'Not a regular Cannabis user, had a bad experience and got stuck in a moment,' he thought, that would get the case moving. There seemed to be no sinister actions here but this guy was messing with some sinister people recently, after what looked like a life in cotton wool. The Coffee Shop and the Dream Bakery had some very 'uncommon' people and the guy Jez had a record that showed he walked a different line. But none of that was illegal, so there was no angle for prosecution.

Wim considered his options. He could turn over the dream bakery and the coffee shop and the residence of Jez, he didn't really have grounds but if he declared it a murder case he would get support from his superiors. The coroner has not given an indication of murder actually he has checked carefully and found no injuries, no sign of struggle, no sub cutaneous marks, looks like Lem Forth walked up to the bench, sat down and never got up. Strange that he did that in the one section of the park that CCTV didn't cover and that he didn't appear on any of the footage from the other camera's. He seems to have wandered all the way around the park to the opposite side from his apartment and sat down, avoiding every known CCTV on the street.

'Uncommon,' that's the word. Not impossible, but uncommon.

His thought train was broken by a call from the corner office.

"Hummel!"

It wasn't so loud that he couldn't ignore it and claim he didn't hear but that call was from his superior and he knew better.

"Hello," Wim said holding onto the door jamb and trying to look friendly. He had been told he always looked grumpy, so he was making an effort in front of those who counted.

"Yes. Hummel. How is your case load? I have another, looks gangland and may take up a lot of your time."

Wim smiled encouragingly, he loved gangland cases.

"It's light he said, just closing off at least four cases, all of them from exposure during the snow the other night."

"Great, show me one." His superior was always forthright in his actions and thorough in his account.

Wim raced back to his desk and picked up the Lem Forth case file returning to lay it on the captain's desk. He waited patiently while his superior read the coroners report, notes from the onsite police investigation and Wim's own notes on the circumstances.

71

"What's the number one reason not to close it," the Superior asked laying his hands on the desk and forming a triangle with his thumbs and his index fingers. Wim didn't want to play it up too much as he wanted to move on to the gangland case but he knew if he didn't play devils advocate, his superior would get him to check closer.

"I could pass this off as a guy who knew little about life finally breaking free of his over protective Aunt, who passed of old age, taking some fairly low level drugs but finding himself caught a moment in our freak weather event."

The superior waited patiently. "But..."

"Yes. But... there are some uncommon elements. For example the stroke was in a section of the brain that rarely suffers and almost never in men so young. The deceased had his keys and a lot of cash on him. The deceased managed to circle to the opposite end of the park and sit on the bench without being caught by one single CCTV camera in the area. The deceased had also been in company of these felons" Wim reached over the desk and pulled out the information sheets on Jez and the coffee shop barista. "I also encountered a particularly shady Australian at the dream bakery that is... as I say, uncommon."

The superior laid his hands flat on the table.

"Unfortunately shady people are not uncommon. I see the report on the owner of the dream bakery and it suggests he has no record and good public standing, a long history with Shell and strong finances. Not the kind of guy that would be murdering." The captain's argument was solid.

"Yes," said Wim "as I said, the case looks closed but there are some uncommon elements I could pursue or not. I may spend another three months turning over rotting wood and find only cockroaches."

"Indeed," the superior took another moment, formed another triangle with his hands and sighed.

"Let's let it rest. If you feel the others are equally worth closing then you may proceed."

"You should read this new ganglang case file and note down anything you think is worth following up. There is a meeting in the large task force room in one hour. You need to be in it as you will be leading the task force."

Wim smiled, maybe it was closing four cases on a Monday morning or maybe it was the surety that his weekends would belong to his work for the foreseeable future.

***

The message from Ruud was not clear but Will didn't need much of an excuse to get out of the Dream Bakery.

'Providing some incoming assistance, but need some help. Interested?'

Eugene was busy with his thing so Will took the quiet exit and headed off to the White House.

Ruud was by the window in his usual spot and Will organised a few beers at the bar from Goos and joined him.

"I have a small job, but a good earner I think," Ruud said in a low voice. "I would do it myself, but I have my obvious affliction." Ruud pointed to his damaged knee with a shrug.

"Great. When." Will knew enough to not ask any other questions. His mind was made up about Ruud. He was shifty but he was also in the thick of it here in Rotterdam and that's where Will wanted to be.

"Let's go after these beers," Ruud said. "There is no hurry but no time like the present."

The two had light conversation around the football and the weather and moved outside. Ruud had a van parked nearby and the two travelled through the Rotterdam streets to the dock where there was a pile of Washing Machines sitting on the dock. Ruud went to talk to the local security guard while Will loaded them into the back of the van and they drove away.

Ruud then drove them to a small lock up where Will again did all the hard work while Ruud busied himself discussing some terms with a guy at a house in the front.

"Right, we are done." Ruud announced as they got into the truck. "Easy money, right?"

Ruud handed over a small roll of twenty Euro notes to Will. Will pondered the ten machines must have been worth a few hundred Euro's each. If they were stolen, he knew that restricted the ability to sell them to probably half, but Ruud appeared to already have a buyer. So it was a small haul easy money. His two hundred Euro's was probably a bit much, but was a sweetener, as they were new friends.

"Not bad for an hour or so," Ruud nodded.

Will continued to ask no questions and just smiled as Ruud parked the van outside the White House.

"Drinks are on me as a bonus," Ruud smiled. Will was always into free drinks.

When they had settled down at Ruud's regular table Will took a moment to gauge Ruud. He didn't trust him, but he didn't need to, he just needed to understand him and watch.

"Normal day or was that something new," Will asked casually. A question like that gave Ruud a hundred ways to answer and provided as much or as little info as he wanted to.

"Yeah," Ruud said with an arrogant sigh. "They are small and boring but low risk. I prefer them a little bigger with a better reward but the truth is they just don't come up often, unless they are drugs and I just don't want to play that game."

Will nodded. He really didn't want to get into any drug dealing. So far he had avoided all of that and he saw no reason to change.

"Well if you need anything else just shout," Will said eagerly. "I'm your man."

"I have another one Thursday. A little larger, probably will take all day." Ruud was looking towards the bar. "I have another guy who will be in as it's too much work for one guy and as much as I would like to, I really can't be trusted to do the physical work."

"Great," Will replied. "You know I'm in."

***

Will slipped off the dream interceptor slowly.

"Geez mate, this dreaming shit is exhausting," he sighed the word exhausting to over dramatise the feeling.

He wasn't even sure Eugene was listening but he knew Daaisi was.

By definition Daaisi could still be 'mate' as the term is all encompassing and whatever you want to identify as, Australians can choose to identify you as 'mate'.

Will got no reply so decided that he should move to the kitchen for a coffee. He knew how to work the machine and the sequence of sleep, dream, coffee must be on one of those inspirational posters somewhere.

He heard the hiss of the milk being lengthened as soon as he opened the door so entered the room with aplomb.

"Another successful mission captain," he cried in a Scottish accent as he walked through the door dipping in a bow to Eugene.

"Way to go," Eugene replied. "What was that last bit?"

Will eyed Eugene. "I said," Will replied with additional dramatics "this dreaming shit is exhausting!"

"Yeah I figured, thus the caffeine," Eugene smiled.

"Seriously, no wonder your testers peter out."

"Interesting observation, Daaisi was Will's physical condition adversely affected during the most recent dream observation."

Will turned his head upward to the speaker in the ceiling in the thought that looking at Daaisi's audio device might illicit a faster response.

"Will's physical condition remains no different than after a standard sleep of a similar nature when no dream observation is being under taken."

Will looked at Eugene with his hands raised to conjure an answer.

"Computer says no," Eugene added.

The two laughed. Eugene moved to the table with two coffees in hand and placed one each in front of two chairs at the table, sitting at one and gesturing Will to take the other.

"So why do I feel so tired?" Will questioned taking his assigned seat and drawing a large draught of coffee.

"That is one of the many things we are here to find out about," Eugene put on his best scientific voice. "Unfortunately these things are not sequential."

The two enjoyed the coffee and made light conversation waiting for Daaisi to conjure up the dream image. At the appropriate moment Eugene asked the million dollar question.

"So do you remember what your dream was about?"

Will looked up sheepishly "Why do I have a feeling you are about to tell me."

"Not just yet," Eugene smiled. "You first."

"Something about escaping or hiding, a long alley way with lots of exits, but I am just running. Not from anyone in particular, more from something."

"OK."

"So what predominant image came through when you woke up, or if you can remember, images or feelings." Eugene had asked these questions many time before but rarely with such care.

"Easy on the feelings," Will laughed, but looked around the room a little apprehensively.

"There was a long tunnel or an alley way or hallway, with tall arched doorways or turns to other hallways or alleyways. It's difficult to recall exactly."

"It takes a lot of practice to remember detail from dreams and even once you feel you have mastered that, recalling those memories is not an exact science." Eugene consoled his friend. "Let's see what Daaisi comes up with."

On cue Daaisi announced the low quality image would be rendered in five minutes.

"Time to get rid of these." Eugene stood and retrieved the dishes and stashed them carefully in the dishwasher drawer.

"Any plans for today," he quizzed.

"Nothing else today. I was thinking of a few quiet beers around here," Will said with a smile.

"Quiet," Eugene laughed, "with you..."

"I have some work tomorrow, supposed to be an all day thing. Might be a good earner."

"Great," Eugene smiled.

"Same guy as yesterday," Will grinned. "I might be onto something big soon."

Eugene eyed his friend, "Nothing too dodgy I hope."

"Nah," Will sassed. "Trust me."

The image did indeed show a long hallway draped in shadows, so it appeared to be a tunnel. It weaved its way throughout the image branching out to form a culvert with a myriad of dead end's, all enveloped in a darkness. The darkness stretched into every corner in a twisted maze which placed one small man at an interval, not even in the centre. Even from this aspect and distance it was clear to see that the man fled in terror even if it wasn't possible to see who, or what, he fled from.

The two men inspected the image quietly before Eugene broke the silence.

"Always an interesting perspective you create."

"Meaning what?" Will replied.

"Meaning most other peoples images, even when they dream of the bigger picture, centre on themselves or someone important to them at the centre-line of the image." Eugene waved his hand in front of the image on the screen. "Yours has you as a dot in the overall scene. Like the seaside picture."

"Not common in my research." Eugene reiterated, "and I am really not sure what that means."

"Can't pin me down," Will smiled.

"Might just be something in that. I'm going to call that research for later as it must be five o'clock somewhere." Eugene had moved to the fridge retrieving two very cold Grolsch bottles.

"Now that's a dream" Will smiled.

***

Kobus was big guy.

By Dutch standards he was a tall guy but by the rest of the worlds standards he was also filled out well to meet his lofty frame. Will was often not fond of big guys, maybe it was an intimidation thing, maybe he had just had poor experiences with them in the past. It certainly wasn't fear. He noticed Kobus seemed relatively placid or perhaps just well under Ruud's spell.

The three of them travelled quietly in the large van. It was rare to find Ruud not in a talkative mood, to Will it seemed that talking was Ruud's nourishment.

The three of them stopped in a side alley off the main dock which had good shielding thanks to a very long line of sea containers. Waiting in that very innocuous place was a large load of kitchen appliances. Somehow, they didn't look out of place. Ruud backed the van in to allow for a quick easy load and Will and Kobus set to work.

It was a reasonable collection and during his very intimate time moving these beautiful Smeg kitchen appliances Will could tell they were fake. Extremely good fakes, but fake they were. Small things, like the safety warning being missing, the inconsistent wrapping and some words spelled wrong. The whole thing was inconsistent when you looked at them in bulk but if you just received one, you just wouldn't notice. Especially if the installer took all the boxes away.

The two of them moved slowly as the appliances were cumbersome and bulky. The medium delivery truck became a big Tetris puzzle into which they needed to fit all the goods. The pickup and drop off took a full five hours, delivery being made this time to a larger warehouse. The three could take no rest on Ruud's insistence but he did pull out some Dutch street food so they could eat.

On leaving, for Will's trouble, he was given one thousand Euros, a bigger smile from Ruud and a new friend in Kobus.

***

Entering the dream bakery with a huge smile it was clear to Eugene that Will's job had gone well.

Eugene's appointment came and went and the routine he had tried to portray worked it's way to a quiet reality. No more police visits, no news saying there was any investigation and the only word out on that particular incident was a local news piece on the fact that seven people died that night showing the atrocious lack of emergency accommodation for the homeless. Eugene saw that as a positive sign he wouldn't be leaving Rotterdam soon, or potentially at all.

He made the transfer of ten thousand Euro's into Will's Crypto account and after a brief conversation and explanation headed back to his private area for some research. He left Will to his own devices promising a return dream session tomorrow or in two days time as he had another test subject in on Thursday.

Will had seemed happy just to hang around, so Eugene felt comfortable he had the afternoon to himself. He wanted to look into dream perspective based on the strange way Will's dreams were appearing as images.

Eugene knew that most people saw dreams from a first person perspective and that sometime people would experience Vicarious dreams, where the dreamer doesn't appear at all, and someone else occupies the first-person perspective. Will's dreams, though, were from a third person perspective, which is rare but not unheard of. Some people suspected that third person became predominant when some part of yourself is being expressed that you cannot accept as being part of yourself. That explanation was a bit complicated, but perhaps fitting with Will's life choices, actions and outcomes. The research Eugene could find was very mixed and a lot of it opinion based and with little underlying research.

That was his constant and most common problem.

Eugene had seen a lot of dream research which didn't follow recognised scientific procedure, it wasn't anything new. That was part of why he was doing this, other scientific studies had PhD thesis, technical outcomes, research and development project papers and a large of body of documentation, but dreams were strongly subjective and rarely tested on those that weren't already listed as mentally impaired or under the influence of some form of narcotic, prescribed or otherwise.

Still feeling the effects of a few days of drinking, Eugene also felt the overwhelming urge to get some sleep under his belt.

***

Will was happy with his stake now. After just a few days in Rotterdam, with the money he had from Eugene he had twelve thousand Euro's. His initial hopes were to build a stake of twenty five thousand, so he could make his way to South America. That should be enough to keep him above ground after he arrived, until he found some other way to generate income.

The ten from Eugene he figured he could turn into fifteen and get Eugene back the money, leaving himself enough to work on for any deals he saw. He figured he was in the right spot hanging out with Ruud and Kobus.

Almost on queue Will received a text message from Ruud.

'Another job is brewing if you have the legs. I will need some help on the stake, hoping you can front. Any chance you can get to the white house for a liquid lunch.'

Will sent the message as he headed out the door.

'On my way'.

The meeting was quick. Ruud needed fifty thousand to secure some electronics but he said he had a buyer. Ruud was clear that normally he would be able to handle it but he outlined he had five payments outstanding so would need ten thousand each from Kobus and Will. Otherwise he would let it go.

"I have it," Kobus was quick to respond. "What's the return?"

"Tomorrow. Stake plus fifty percentage return." Ruud rubbed his hands together to allow the action to emphasise the high return.

'Fifty!' Will thought, 'nice'.

"Whats the risk," Will asked.

"The pickup is very low risk, almost the same as yesterday." Ruud looked over his shoulder out of the window. Will had been in many of these planning meetings and to him that action was a bad sign. The drop off is not one of my regulars, to be honest we will need to be on alert."

Kobus smiled. He knew that was why he was here. The muscle.

Ruud looked across at Will, "if ten is too much we can cancel."

"It's no problems, if you think it's worthwhile. You have a stake I assume." He returned Ruud's stare, not an accusation but a summing up of character between two men who knew such things were all front.

"I'm in for thirty, the deal is fifty in seventy five out. So we split by stake. I think that is reward for risk. We don't want to be caught with these goods."

"No drugs," Kobus grunted.

"Brother you know me," Ruud said. "None of that."

"Do we get to know?" Will questioned.

"Not now. But hold your money. On pickup if it's too much we can back away then."

Will was surprised, that is not the normal way of things. "When," he asked.

Ruud's reply went a long way to explain to Will what was going on.

"I need to get some cash, back here in an hour, if you can do it. Goods are on the dock waiting, if we don't get there another crew will jump in, but my guy says we have first go. Drop off needs to be immediate but the money return is twenty four hours after the goods make the final destination."

The three agreed.

Will went straight to a Bitcoin ATM he had scoped out earlier and sold the coins Eugene had sent him. Ten thousand seven hundred Euros giving him a bonus seven hundred Euro's made in a morning of doing nothing. Will smiled but he knew Bitcoin was not the way to make his stake and that ten thousand seven hundred would be nine thousand three hundred tomorrow and who knew what by next Monday. The ATM was only fifteen minutes from the white house so he stopped on the way back to get a quick bite to eat. So far his experience was that this would be hard work moving stuff and Kobus was a beast on his end so Will needed some energy, after all he wasn't getting any younger. When he got back to the White House with ten minutes to spare Ruud was waiting in a truck outside. Kobus arrived five minutes later and the three of them headed out.

The pickup location was as before on the dock. This time the goods were housed in a large sea container lost in the maze of other sea containers. Ruud had the details and unlike all the others this one was unlocked. Ruud took extra precautions not stopping outside the target and looping around twice, allowing Will and Kobus to double check any unwanted eyes or anything suspicious. Nothing was evident so they proceeded inside.

"Drones," Will said quietly. "Not quite what I expected."

"Competition drones," Kobus reiterated with a surprised tone.

"Headed for Ukraine," Ruud whispered.

Will and Kobus looked at each other.

"Not at all illegal, but this shipment is way over quota. We drop in two places and from there it's under quota, that is our cut. So are we in."

Both men nodded.

"That would be cash to confirm," Ruud smiled.

Kobus handed his ten thousand over, notes clearly from other jobs in a variety of denominations and time on the street.

Will's crisp clean ATM notes looked out of place by comparison. Ruud added them to a bag he had which he showed both men had his stake in it.

The load went smoothly with Kobus and Will working in unison to get the goods loaded while Ruud busied himself outside on watch. Within two hours the job was done and the three of them were in the truck on the way to the first drop off.

Ruud looked nervous to Will, which was a good thing. If this was breaching EU military import rules the justice would be harsh and it was clear the drop was a little unknown to Ruud. At the moment they were all very complicit but Ruud would bear the brunt of any incarceration as Will and Kobus knew nothing.

Will was happy for the rest and thankful he took the time to eat earlier. Kobus was indeed, a machine and was just sitting back enjoying the ride while Will recuperated. The drop off was a bit out of Rotterdam, almost to The Hague on the outskirts near the small coastal town of Monster. The shed was attached to a long string of greenhouses, hard to know one from the other but it seemed to Will that Ruud knew the way.

The first drop off went without a hitch and within another half an hour they turned into the loading area of a small warehouse in the south of Leiden. Ruud met a guy in the front while Kobus and Will offloaded. When the job was done Ruud met them with a smile saying it was all in place. The two shipments are due to be passed on tonight and we will be very well compensated tomorrow.

It was a long day and Will was exhausted. Ruud suggested a few beers at the white house but Will declined saying he had something else on with another guy that night. He didn't want Ruud to think he was his only income avenue, that never sat well with confidence guys. When the truck pulled up Will headed back to the Dream Bakery and headed straight to sleep.

He was shattered.

***

Eugene's sleep was short and broken.

He was thankful there was no pink snake and no third person perspective in his dreaming. His reading was great for his conscious and he had filled in a lot of blanks around Will's crazy perspective thanks to some great research done by Turkish psychiatrists.

"Is Will in the Dream Bakery," he enquired of the ever present Daaisi?

"No Eugene. Will left at 11:45 am and has not returned."

Eugene took another moment to check if there was any further fallout from Lem's death. Daaisi had been compiling articles that might be associated and he worked his way through that list discounting all those avenues.

Eugene had already decided he would eventually need to leave Rotterdam. He was pretty sure, even if nothing came of the Police action, that it would be a good preventative step to keep his record clean, giving the police no reason to pursue him. His intention was to leave to Dream Bakery in a functional state, but he would ensure everything to do with his research was taken offsite.

His plan involved moving things around for an hour a day, then moving some of the furniture from his own living quarters into a room on first floor so it looked like it was his living quarters. The non clandestine part of the second floor was mostly empty so he relocated a conference table into that area and made it appear like it was used infrequently for meetings. He needed to make sure if he wasn't here and anyone arrived they would see a market research company recently shutdown because of the financial situation. The plan included some detailed losses that would be added to the books. Some customers that no longer needed his services and some unexpected costs that meant the business was just not viable.

It was an elaborate plan, but that was Eugene.

"Will has returned to the Dream Bakery" Daaisi's voice blended into the silence of Eugene's private quarters. "He has gone directly to interview room one and is preparing to sleep."

Eugene decided that might be for the best and turned his attention back some of the background reference material of the Turkish dream researchers. It was fascinating what they had found from the five hundred or so people they had surveyed. finally the world was reserching dreams in an organised fashion.

***

The day within the Dream Bakery didn't dawn. Daaisi had strict control over the light and the sounds of the outside and unless instructed otherwise. It was always the optimal light for sight and the optimal silence for hearing as per the parameters Daaisi had either been explicitly provided or from research from internet sources verified by Eugene. Daaisi had subroutines that aimed for continual self improvement but parameters like light and sound didn't vary much and so had not really been updated or changed since those subroutines were first initiated.

Will woke in a bit of a daze.

Another strange dream, what was it about this place. This one left him trapped but not in the large maze he had last time but under the arm of a giant. A huge scarred and tattooed arm which pinned his neck onto the floor with a high level of force. It was not painful but his generally feeling was one of discomfort. Before that, the day bed had been very comfortable to sleep on.

"Coffee will fix it," he thought.

"Hey doll, is Eugene around?" he said looking up at the rooftop speaker as was his most effective communication method with Daaisi.

"Eugene is in his private quarters monitoring the test subject in interview room two," Daaisi smoothly informed.

"Perfect," Will said out loud before heading to the bathroom.

His business finished Will headed to the kitchen for some coffee returning quickly with a fresh black coffee for maximum effect. He had checked his phone three times since waking up hoping for something from Ruud, but now he had a moment sent a quick message.

'Any news on the return?'

The coffee hit the spot and feeling a little more awake he headed back to the bathroom for a shower.

The shower in the Interview Room was a minimalist effort employing just the basic shower head, screen and taps but it was effective and the hot water soothed a few muscles that were complaining after yesterdays effort. By the time he was finished and dry Will felt almost ready to face the world.

Still nothing from Ruud.

Not wanting to bother Eugene he thought he would head back to the White House to talk to Ruud in person or at least get a beer or two before lunch.

He was pretty hungry and had notice the White House had a pretty good pub menu. He could kill for a steak sandwich.

Ruud wasn't in the White House.

He made his way to the bar and behind it was a guy he hadn't met before. Will ordered a tap beer and steak sandwich and asked if it was Goos' day off or if he was on later. The guy behind the bar said he didn't know Goos so Will just let it go and went to the table Ruud would usually occupy.

The meal came and he ate quickly. He was famished. On his second trip to the bar he enquired further about Goos or if the guy behind the bar knew Ruud. The bartender said he didn't know a Goos or a Ruud but that he worked everyday except Wednesdays and Thursdays and on those days Wilma was supposed to be at that particular bar.

Will was a little surprised and worked back in his mind what days it was he had been here. They were indeed only Wednesday's and Thursday's. That spread a little panic through him and we all know it only takes a little panic to spread like wildfire. Will called the number he had for Ruud which showed as not connected. He called Kobus, also not connected. He headed back to the dream bakery and asked Eugene if he could use his car. In a wild game of chance he back tracked to all the places he could remember but there was nothing, either his memory let him down or the places held no trace of anything related.

He did get one lead, remembering the precise location of the first drop off warehouse but there was no-one around. In desperation, Will broke in, but the area was empty and nothing he found lead him to believe a Ruud or a Kobus or a Will had ever been there before.

Dejected, Will headed back to the dream bakery.

He knew he had been conned.

Chapter Seven

The Moment Thief

Will wasn't sure how to broach the subject of the con he had fallen for with Eugene. He had time to make the money again and return it without alarming his friend. He had certainly not given up and didn't want to give anything away just yet.

The two sat quietly preparing for Will's third and, on Eugene's insistence, final dream session.

"I think it should be last because I'm just not sure on the effects and don't want to be experimenting on you," Eugene laughed.

"But I'm loving it," Will teased.

"If it works out okay, maybe you can have another go in a week or two," Eugene added.

"Okay Dad," Will laughed.

"Daaisi please deliver ten thousand volts through the dream interceptor attached to will-i-used-to-be." Eugene delivered the sentence as a perfect straight forward order.

Will looked nervous for a moment until Daaisi cut in.

"The dream interceptor is not equipped with a voltage delivery system Eugene."

Eugene smiled, "'she' would have done it," he said emphasising the 'she'.

"Very funny," Will lay back and closed his eyes. "You go and make yourself useful and warm up that coffee machine."

Finally left alone with his thoughts Will slept very quickly and as was his situation Will dreamed he was truly trapped.

This time, not by giant arms or in a maze but in a glass cage. On the outside a wide range of people and creatures taunted him. Some poking him with sharp objects. His body slowly bleeding, with the blood dripping and congealing, littering the bottom of his cage. The taunting, poking, beating proceeded to a drum beat slowly giving the perpetrators time to rest and faster to provide the back beat to a frenzied attack. As the blood increased Will felt more and more distraught, his energy level declining and his consciousness in the dream fading.

Just as Will was ready to pass out, the blood in the cage formed into an Octopus. Not very large and with a normal brownish-green colour, it looked at him imploringly. As they do, the octopus reached its tentacle into one of the holes used by the taunting crowd, gripping the next hole closest from the outside and pulling its entire body through the first very small hole. It stopped momentarily when its large head reached the hole and squeezed its head into a cylinder around its eyes to ensure they went through.

As the drum beat began to quicken, the Octopus, now fully outside the glass box and on the floor of the warehouse looked at him again with a sense of urgency. Will tried the same manouver, reaching into an unused hole and pushing with his finger to grip the next available hole. Crazy as it seemed, Will was able to compress his entire body into the hole and reaching and gripping with his elongated fingers squeezed his body up to his neck into the hole before becoming stuck as it was clear his skull couldn't compress. In that moment he woke up coughing and spluttering.

"Water is available in a small cupboard underneath the side table within easy reach of you. Please take a moment before you stand up." Daaisi's voice was clear and concise and on autopilot Will reached down under the side table and drank the contents of the first bottle. His throat was on fire.

"Eugene is currently in the kitchen area," Daaisi stated. "Your physical condition appears to be adversely affected Will-I-used-to-be. Should I alert Eugene that you are in need of some assistance."

"No." Will's hoarse voice could only manage the one word, but it was enough. He reached in for the second bottle and slowly sipped the contents and regained his composure.

'What was that?' he thought. "That will be the last of those for sure," he confirmed to himself out loud.

Will took a moment, recovering but still feeling a little groggy. He finished the second bottle of water and even though he knew it was in vain he checked his messages.

Finally getting to his feet he headed to the bathroom to wash his face and run some cold water over his head which was wet with sweat. Still with the bathroom towel in his hand he headed for the kitchen.

The smell of fresh coffee grounds met him halfway down the hall and the familiar scream of the milk being lengthened meant Eugene was already on the job. As he entered the room Will was presented with a nod to the chair from Eugene and met at the chair with a large cup of hot latte.

"Looked like you might need a large one," Eugene added. "That looked less than ideal."

"What is going on in there?" Will bawled.

"I said it was going to be the last one" Eugene added "and now there is no doubt. Daaisi recorded some breathing anomalies, a severe temperature drop, a heart-rate bpm drop and some pre-ischemic activity which passed quickly, but are a concern."

"A Concern," Will shrieked.

"Mate, more than a concern." Eugene was trying to keep a hold of things but was not doing very well.

"What did that last guy die of?" Will added.

"The police just said a heart attack so I don't have any more information."

"You should get some more information before you experiment further," Will was beside himself.

"Do you feel any dizziness or numbness anywhere? You don't seem to have any confusion, so there are no medical signs of..."

Will cut him off.

"No medical signs," he was not impressed. "What was with the octopus?"

"Octopus?" Eugene asked.

"Yeah, made out of my blood, slipped out through one of the holes in the cage."

"Have you seen an octopus in your dreams before?" Eugene asked.

"No," Will replied shortly. "But there he was looking at me like he knew stuff, like a way out and I should follow suit, so I did and almost suffocated."

"But you didn't suffocate," Eugene added.

"Obviously," Will replied sarcastically. "But it felt like I was going to."

"That was pretty intense and it all happened so fast. I was monitoring what information we get during these sessions and you seemed fine right up until the last moment."

"Fine!" Will exploded. "Not fine, that was a particularly nasty dream."

"Sorry mate. Tell me," Eugene said gently.

Will explained the contents in as much detail as he could. He couldn't make out the people or even if some of them were people, they were shapes, spectre's, smudges or collections of variations of things. Something that looked like a knitting needle with legs and arms, a sort of balloon with teeth, a smudged playing card with laser red eyes.

Eugene sat quietly listening.

"The initial render will be available in five minutes." Daaisi's voice wafted over the kitchen. "Twenty three percent of the render has only achieved a sixty seven percent match."

"What does that mean?" Will asked Eugene.

"It means Daaisi has nothing to match what you dreamed in any of her known sources so should just fills in the blanks with blurred contents matching the image surrounds. Best we have a look and see what it means."

Eugene took a moment to consider.

"The octopus is most likely an animal totem," Eugene added. "Like my pink snake."

"Animal totem," Will said drily.

"Yes," Eugene followed on. "The octopus is actually a good match for you. Resourceful, adaptable, intelligent, creative, mysterious, able to navigate complex situations and built for defence and protection, not attack. Sound like you?" Eugene raised his eyebrows to form a question.

"So it was looking out for me," Will asked?

"Most people who believe in such things, believe so. But my own experience with an Animal Totem has been very frustrating."

"The bugger had a look on his face, assuming that was a he, like he wanted me to do something that would help the situation I was in. He demonstrated it and then egged me on." Will felt a bit silly talking this way, but of all the people in the world he could have this conversation with, Eugene would be at the top of the list.

"Jury is still out but that is very interesting," Eugene replied. "I have read many accounts of people experiencing dream totem animals. The 'totem' could refer to a person or thing with symbolic importance. It didn't have to be an animal, but for some reason animals come up a lot. In totemism, a totem is a spirit-being that's believed to have a mystical relationship"

The render appeared on the kitchen monitor unannounced and the two of them studied it carefully. Will was again shown in the third person. The picture showed him clearly in a glass cage towards the bottom of the left hand quadrant of an overall picture of a large warehouse. There are holes in the cage with sharp implements poking through some of the holes from one side. The people or spirits or shapes or whatever were obscured by the octopus who is looking directly at Will allowing only the side on expression to be seen but it would be easy to call it an impassioned expression.

"You must be kidding me," Will cried.

"What's that?" Eugene queried him.

"The warehouse. Where did you get that picture?" Will's face had fallen to despair.

"Do you know it," Eugene asked?

"I was there. Yesterday." Will stood up take a closer look. Somewhere near Leiden. How can she know?"

"Like I said, Daaisi just joins the dots, so to speak," Eugene added.

"The other stuff is very subjective. My memory of the dream might be influenced by events, but the picture of that warehouse is almost spot on. Straight from what I remember from yesterdays trip."

"Not worth the pain but that is something amazing. So what was the octopuses point?" Will was looking like he either needed another coffee, a beer or maybe something stronger.

"Based on what you have said, he is your spirit animal and he was trying to help. He showed you a way out, a way to break away from what is holding you back. Maybe it was something you couldn't achieve in your current state so he was encouraging you to change. I would say he was your brains or your sub conscious' response to whatever else was happening, in an attempt to steal the moment that was fast approaching from threatening your life."

"Right so this saviour, this moment thief, is he coming back tonight for more?" Will looked a little nervous.

"I wish I knew," Eugene looked down. "My own pink snake only came out when the dream interceptor was attached, it was the same for Paige."

"Wait, she had a totem too." Will gave Eugene a look like the whole story needed to come out.

"Yeah. Same as mine." Eugene gave a half awkward smile.

"Same as yours? What about the guy that died." Will was not smiling.

"Yeah, he saw it too, same token. With him I kept pushing, to fight past it blocking any detail and in the end I got what I needed."

"and he died..." Will said impassively. "Mate you are dealing with some bad JuJu here, must be time to back away."

Eugene picked up the empty coffee cups. "We might need something stronger than coffee," he said.

Eugene looked up at the screen deep into the eyes of the imploring octopus.

"The Moment Thief. I like that."

***

Adrie was feeling a little scatty when she woke up. She had some strange variations in her dreams that had woken her up several times through the night, or maybe it was Douglas. He had been home a few weeks but she still couldn't get used to his fidgeting. He was healing and seemed to be resting well. He hadn't been working, as far as she could see, but Sam and John had been putting pressure on him to return. They would often say no pressure, but can you answer this question. They just didn't see that hearing the question and talking through something were almost as bad as doing it, especially where his blood pressure and his heart were concerned. He often needed the rest of the day to get over those invasive conversations but they would just be back the next day, unless she put her foot down.

She tried to have him available for questions only twice a week not everyday. Douglas was pretty tough and seemed okay but there was no doubt he shouldn't be answering on any days. His doctor had reiterated no work and maximum rest. The doctor was very clear he thought Douglas was not okay. He had placed Douglas on some very strong drugs to lower the impact of life, so Douglas could heal, not so Douglas could work through.

So this new life hit a routine. Her trying to keep him relaxed and happy and everyone else, including Douglas himself, trying to stress him out.

Adrie had been nervous all week to get back to see another view of her dream.

She had emailed the dream photographer to ask to move the appointment to an earlier date but he had replied, or maybe it was the AI, that no other appointment times were available.

She tried to meditate hoping to gain some patience, unfortunately that just made her more anxious as she thought about nothing else while she was freeing her mind of everything. So between cleaning and looking after Douglas and trying to forget, she had no time to chat to her friends and so they bombarded her with questions about why she hadn't called them. They all wanted to know about her last visit and see her photograph. So her avoidance could only last so long or maybe not, if she continued to blame Douglas. Seemed to be working so far and after today she would know more and hopefully be able to say more.

On her last visit she found the white cap, the dream interceptor, quite tight and annoying. She tried a different hair approach this week going with a more free flowing style, no gels or firming creme or spray. To match that, she went with a more relaxed dress option with some jeans and a loose collared shirt with a pastel striped pattern on it.

The day was clear but a strong biting wind rose up from the east. Adrie had supplemented her casual attire with a jacket but she hoped the wind didn't push in a storm as none of it had any water resistance. She could always Uber it home if she needed to.

The Dream Bakery walk helped to refresh her mind and today was no different, except her mind was usually not needing much attention and was happy and free. Today it was not. So the walk just added to her frustration in not being able to properly order her thoughts. This was exacerbated by her taking a wrong turn and having to back track along one of the canals. She was born in Rotterdam and knew its roads and canals backwards, so what was that all about.

When the building came into sight she almost cried. Not the reaction she would expect or usually have.

'Just dreams pet,' she consoled herself.

She rang the bell and without a word being said heard the click of the door unlocking. AI is a little rude she thought, some form of introduction or welcome was surely in order. She pushed on the door and made her way into the servery.

"Good Morning Adrie". Daaisi's smooth English accent flooded the room with a cheery tone.

Adrie rolled her eyes, it was the AI.

"Yes, Good Morning. Is Eugene available for our appointment. Sorry, I am a little early."

"Yes, Eugene will be here shortly. Would you like some refreshments? Please help yourself from the refrigerator on your left."

"No thank you," Adrie was not ready to start a conversation with the AI so waited patiently standing in the servery.

"It looks like it is getting quite cold outside." Daaisi said calling on her conversational subroutines to assist Adrie to pass the time as instructed. "The report is for rain. May I enquire if you have covered transport for your journey home."

"No pet. I walked here." Adrie admonished herself for calling the AI pet.

"If you like I can arrange you some alternative transportation home." Daaisi was not being helpful, she was following a pre-developed subroutine that she had seen in other literature and had approved by Eugene.

"Let's see shall we," Adrie deliberately closed off the conversation and pulled out her personal device to look at something. Anything would do.

A few minutes passed as Daaisi continued her default, silent subroutine.

Eugene broke the silence with an apology for his tardiness.

"I was caught on a call with a colleague that went over time," he said. His excuse sounded plausible but the truth was he was moving some equipment around, doing more on his internal organisation and things were a bit heavier than he thought so it took him a while longer.

"No problems pet," Adrie replied walking towards the interview room. "You are my only appointment today. Just need to get back later to look after my husband."

"Is he okay?" Eugene enquired.

"Oh pet, I didn't tell you before. He recently had a heart attack, nearly died and has been at home with me for a few weeks now." Her face fell a little.

"He is tougher than he looks but I worry he will return too work to quickly. He eats poorly and too much when he is working and he doesn't care for himself well. I would like to travel with him but he always seems to like to travel alone and travel appears to be so much of the work he does."

She turned to face Eugene in the doorway of the interview room.

"What can we do, eh."

Eugene nodded. "What work does your husband do?" he asked

"Electronics & Technology. He is the CEO of a startup industrial safety company. For years he was just running technology services, part of me wishes he had stuck to that."

Adrie reached down and retrieved the dream interceptor which was placed on the day bed. She fitted the device and sat down.

"Does the seam feel better?" Eugene asked. "I made some changes after our last conversation. Truth is you are not the first person to complain of some discomfort."

Adrie looked up with a smile. "Oh my, you listened."

"Of course," Eugene replied.

"Feels great now, lets see how we go." Adrie reclined to a more comfortable position.

"I will be in the kitchen when the session is done," he said retreating to the door.

***

Adrie woke with a jolt.

"What just happened," she thought.

She knew it was important to try to collect your thoughts of the dream as soon as you wake up so the subconscious memory is not swamped by the all encompassing thoughts of the conscious.

There was that room again. She couldn't see anyone except Douglas but the whole room oozed sex. There was steam and passion and oil, the light was low and the music, was that Bolero or a modern version with keyboards. There was a lot of action but she couldn't see any of it, just some parts that were unmistakably Douglas and then a beaver.

She propped herself up on the daybed and then took a sitting position placing her bare feet on the cold floor.

A beaver. There was definitely a beaver and she was building a wall. A female beaver. How did Adrie even know what was the difference between a male and a female beaver.

Strange.

Adrie went to stand up and unable to balance, fell back onto the bed.

"Water is available in a small cupboard underneath the side table within easy reach of you. There is no need to stand up." Daaisi's voice was clear and concise.

"I'm okay," Adrie lied. "I just lost my footing."

"Please take a moment to rest and hydrate." Daaisi instructed, "you have been asleep for over four hours."

Adrie did not want to take any instruction from an AI, but it did seem a wise course of action.

She finished half the small bottle of water and felt much improved. Her second attempt to get to her feet was successful and she made her way towards the door with thoughts of what wonder awaited her in the kitchen.

"Are you okay," Eugene enquired when she entered?

"Yes pet. A little unsteady at first just needed a moment. That was longer than I slept in the other sessions."

"It was," said Eugene. "In my experience that can vary so nothing to worry about. Have a seat and please let me know anything you can recall while I finish making the coffee."

"A beaver," Adrie blurted out. "I don't know what that was about but there was a very sassy looking female beaver."

"Really." said Eugene turning his attention from the coffee process to Adrie for a moment. "That is interesting. Tell me more."

"How does a beaver get into that hotel room scene. It was the same as last time, smelling of sex and smoke and feeling like passion and heat, very hot and then a beaver."

"Very curious," Eugene added. "So was anyone else in the hotel room with the beaver?"

"It felt like Douglas, my husband." Adrie replied, "but to be honest, the beaver was blocking the view. That sounds so ridiculous but that is what I recall."

"OK." Eugene stated authoritatively. "That does now make some more sense. I have seen similar in other test cases."

"Really," Adrie said amazed. "Beavers!"

"No not beavers," Eugene patted the air in a motion to calm down.

His preparation complete he moved the two cups of coffee over to the table.

"Oh never have I needed this so much," Adrie exclaimed.

"The low quality image would be rendered in five minutes," Daaisi announced.

Adrie took her time to really enjoy the total coffee experience. She allowed the steam rising from the cup to drift over her face breathing gently and savouring the sensation. She touched the cup to test the heat and turned the handle to allow her to place a gentle grip and raise the cup slowly to her mouth where she took another deep breath. The sensation of smell and touch complete, it was time for the contents. Adrie didn't rush, she sipped at the coffee pushing the nutty liquid slowly over her tongue before swallowing and breathing again to absorb the subtle aftertaste.

"A beaver," she said again. Clearly her mind had been wandering as she enjoyed her coffee on autopilot.

"Tell me about the beaver," Eugene enquired. "You said it was female."

"How do I know that?" she replied. "I don't know much about beavers but it felt like a female, something within me just knew."

"That can happen in dreams." Eugene consoled Adrie, "especially if the beaver is a dream totem."

"A what," Adrie snapped.

"A dream animal to help you, understand or navigate or adapt or explain. It can be a different experience for everyone."

"Oh." Adrie stopped and took a moment to rejoin her coffee experience, which seemed so much simpler.

"So it's there to take care of me in my dreams? Are dreams that dangerous that I need a carer?" Adrie wasn't being sarcastic. She found herself not really understanding what all this was about.

"It's not that simple, some people believe they are more than a carer." Eugene was very happy that the image scrolled onto the screen in the kitchen, "more like a guide."

The image was indeed of the same hotel room, this time from an alternative perspective as Eugene, or my precisely Daaisi had scripted. The picture was smokey and dimly lit, with various pieces of clothing littering the visible furniture. Most prominent was the bed with a large man with his back to the camera perspective. This time the upper body of the person, which should have been clearly visible from this perspective had been blocked by a wooden dam built by the very camera friendly beaver which was peering forward as if to scold the watcher for looking in on this very private scene.

Eugene was sitting, looking a little bit unsure how to proceed explaining this to Adrie. Lucky for him Adrie was also lost for words.

Adrie was also considering how much harder it was going to be to explain this picture to her friends with a beaver in it, on top of the last picture.

More to the point she was thinking about how to avoid telling or showing anyone at all.

***

"What is no further sessions for the foreseeable future suppose to mean." Adrie shrieked as she glared furiously at the email on her tablet. "I bet it's that AI."

The email had sent her the high resolution image of her last session but terminated any future sessions, pending some changes being made to the processes and equipment.

She dearly wanted to continue and push past the crazy beaver to see who Douglas was having sex with. The two of them had barely spoken since she first realised what her dream was trying to tell her. She had done some snooping but with Douglas at home and glued to his electronic devices there was no avenue to go beyond checking his clothes.

The picture was clearly not her and the constant repetition of the room he is in means it is not a one off. It looked a bit like a hotel room but had some items in it that meant it was likely more than a hotel. Did he have a place she didn't know about? He certainly had the finances to fund something like that. She had read stories of men who have whole other lives, even children with other women that their wife didn't know about.

Adrie investigated the picture intently, with particular care around the periphery of what the beaver was trying to block. There was a bookshelf to the left of the bed, but the books were not distinguishable. There was some electronic devices but they were not Douglas's and not known to her. On the end was what looked like a hair scrunchy but could just be some random fabric.

To the right of the bed was a side table and a lamp. The side table had a glass, presumably just water some tissues and some keys. She wondered at how her mind came up with this detail. She had never been to this place. There was nothing to give away anything.

Adrie took a moment to look back at the previous image. The bedside table was there but no tissues and no glass, but there was a handbag she missed when she look at the image last time.

She needed to talk to Eugene about this. She replied to the email asking for some time to discuss the previous two images. She was secretly hoping he would suggest a discussion over coffee but she would be happy with a phone call.

Adrie moved into the kitchen to make some tea.

She could see Douglas in the sitting room reading from his tablet. He spent so much time away from her and lately, with this new venture so much time away from Rotterdam he certainly had the time. He was very active when he was at home, to her he was a good and attentive lover and he treated her so well she felt like his queen. This was not what she though happened when a relationship was in trouble.

Her tablet let out a triumphant ring to notify her that an email had been received. It was from the Dream Photographer, more likely it was from his AI. It was a beautifully constructed email with a very suitable pleasantries and detail provided with perfect delivery of tone and timing. Those things were important to Adrie.

She replied confirming a ten a.m. tomorrow appointment at the dream bakery. It wasn't explicitly dictated but a meeting at that time would imply coffee would be served.

Perfect.

Adrie sipped her rose hip tea and tried hard to relax. She couldn't look at Douglas again and decided the keep herself busy by cleaning the upstairs while he was busy downstairs.

***

The coffee was its usual high quality. He was so consistent with his coffee, better than most of the cafe's that Adrie would visit.

"I do understand you are doing research and I also understand that you are at a point in your research where you need to make some changes and that will take some time."

She was trying to bring the conversation to her needs but not feeling like she was doing it very well.

"I just was hoping we could have another session to better uncover what is in my recurring picture. I don't mind to use the old way and the old technology."

"That's not advisable. I would be in breach of my duty of care," Eugene argued.

Adrie almost laughed. "You have a duty of care."

"Did you read the NDA?" Eugene quizzed.

"OK," Adrie said not wanting to argue. "Do you think once you are back up and running you can add me to your appointment list?"

"Of course," he added. "At the moment I would estimate that to be about a month."

Adrie's face fell. "OK" she sighed. "Can you help me with some of this information from my other two pictures."

"Sure. Let's put the first image on the big screen." The large image of Douglas' back came up on the screen.

Adrie sighed.

"I am particularly interested in two points. The bedside table has some items on it but I cant make out any detail. I am pretty sure they don't belong to Douglas."

Eugene had noticed that Adrie didn't like Daaisi being in the conversation so he was operating things from his wireless keyboard and mouse. He zoomed in on the bedside table and enhanced the image.

"I would say that's a makeup compact and a lipstick in front of a small makeup bag. How about you?" Eugene stood up and pointed to the enhanced image.

"Yes, That's it" Adrie replied "Can we zoom further?"

"I can only try." Eugene manipulated the image according.

Adrie had become much more interested now and moved little closer to the screen.

"Do you think the colours are accurate?" she asked Eugene. "That is a red make up bag with white writing, would that be from my memory?" She looked a little closer.

"That design is not one I am familiar with, the letters are script writing and it says..." she stopped to get a closer inspection. "It appears to say 'rods'. Let me check and see if I can see a rods brand" Adrie took out her personal device and proceeded to use the web browser to search for 'rods' makeup.

Eugene took an alternative approach and from the prompt ask Daaisi to match from the picture and display the result to the screen.

"A Harrods makeup bag," he said triumphantly.

"Ah," Adrie said "I have never had one of those but that puts us squarely in London or with someone from London. Thank you Eugene."

"The picture isn't necessarily a complete re-creation of an actual event," Eugene reiterated.

"Yes. I understand, but it's all I have to go on."

The two of them found little else in the pictures to work with. The Harrods makeup bag was not in the second picture and the keys had nothing to link them with anyone. She knew they did not belong to Douglas.

"There is an outside possibility this is just your suspicions and there is nothing going on," Eugene reiterated.

"Yes pet, I know. But maybe this is my subconscious telling me I should check, just in case," she replied shrugging her shoulders. "I will do some more snooping around until you get your changes made and then hopefully we can get past the crazy beaver."

"Has the beaver been in any of your dreams since this image was rendered," Eugene asked?

"Surprisingly no," Adrie replied. "I have thought of nothing else since I first laid eyes on her but she hasn't appeared in my dreams again. I have been stuck in this room in many ways for a long time, last night though it was empty, and I mean completely empty in perfect order with the bed made and the shelves dusted and cleaned. I walked into the en-suite and it was immaculate. I really don't know what that means."

"Sorry to say I don't either but we have uncovered something I would be happy to pursue in a few weeks and I will get Daaisi to setup an appointment as soon as we have tested out our changes."

"Great" Adrie added. "Thank you for taking the time and the lovely coffee. Sorry if I seem a little neurotic. My husband is quite unwell and I think this might be leading me somewhere to explain some things. I can see myself out."

Adrie exited the dream bakery and took the long walk home. She needed a moment to think, mostly how she was going to deal with Douglas. She did love him and just couldn't believe he was seeing anyone else. The images had rocked her to her core.

She thought about presenting it to him, to hopefully elicit some form of explanation. But she could almost imagine his reaction, especially on the second image with the big inquisitive beaver staring at him.

No, she would instead play a business as usual around Douglas. She would check what financial records and receipts she could find for anything from Harrods and also anything she could find on any apartments or accommodation he had in London. The second one would be tricky as they would be work receipts and Douglas had those electronically, in a system she had no access to.

The sunset beckoned her in the distance, to walk a little further and think a little more. Adrie had never been one just to keep her own company but this was all beyond anything she felt she could explain to anyone else. The light was fading fast as she opened the front door. Douglas was in the cinema room watching an old John Wayne western movie in Black and White. He had seemed to be fulfilling his part of the deal and he gave her a very sleepy sounding hello as she walked in. She had planned to make him a quinoa salad for dinner and had most of it ready to complete so she poured herself a large glass of wine and sat in the sun room looking out over the back garden as the night embraced the world.

Chapter Eight

A Friend in Need

Adrie had again left a tray of food outside the study door.

Douglas didn't understand what he had done wrong or why Adrie was being so difficult, or maybe he did, but he didn't know how she knew. The first few days or even first two weeks she had been so lovely and attentive and thoughtful. Then she seemed to change her tune, maybe once it was clear he was going to live. His health was definitely improving, a good combination of the salads, the lower stress and getting as much sleep as his brain would allow.

He looked down to check his laces, feeling good he could finally wear shoes again, even if they were only his indoor shoes.

Adrie seemed pretty annoyed anytime he took on anything that looked like work, truth is that was probably a good thing. He had been happy at first to just get critical information back to Paul and answer stupid questions twice a week from Big Sam and Johnno but it was almost a month now and there were somethings he was pretty sure only he could do. The two of them didn't even seem to try to understand and so how could they conceivably make informed decisions. Without Paul the whole thing would have fallen apart in the first week.

There was no replacement in Sales for Amber and while Sam thought he could handle it, his real solution was to pass it over to his super capable wife Joanne. She was up to the job, amongst the three thousand other things he had her doing while looking after their three kids. To Douglas, and probably to her, it all seemed a bit unfair.

Douglas felt he could sneak a few of those things in to help out and it wouldn't affect him too badly. He changed his reading from relaxing stuff to stuff that was more industrial or more work focused. He could do it in his own time, sleep if he wanted, it seemed a low stress way to help out. He would then summarise it and send relevant stuff to Paul to disseminate to the team. The problem was when Sam found out he was 'back on the tools', Sam saw it as a chance to heap more of the work Sam was supposed to be doing onto Douglas. So his work queue went from answering questions internally to dealing with issues and answering queries direct from potential customers.

There were a few moments when he had to back out. Some of the prescription medications he had made him quite lethargic, if they didn't outright put him to sleep. He needed to have a least an hour in the morning and an hour in the afternoon to rest after the big green tablets. They had a detrimental effect particularly on his ability to focus. Focus had always been one of Douglas' great strengths and the inability to focus was particularly irritating.

As Adrie wasn't really discussing much with him, he did all of this without her knowing. Mostly he thought this was a good idea, her knowledge of anything he was doing would just worry her and then there would be trouble amongst Adrie, Big Sam and Johnno. There were no money issues, he could close the whole organisation down if he needed and they would still be fine. It would be just OK and Douglas never wanted to be just OK.

Sam, Johnno and Douglas were friends. Sam and Johnno were friends from primary school and Douglas turned up in High School. It was well passed thirty years they had spent as friends, some travel, a lot of drinking, hunting, fishing, watching sport and a myriad of other things guys get up to. Christmas days and birthdays followed by weddings and kids birthdays as they aged. Douglas was always a little bit different, he was white collar while Sam was inherently blue collar, with Johnno switching between the two. Johnno often installed himself in the white collar position of a blue collar industry, rising through the ranks quickly or running organisations that consulted or advised.

When Big Sam had 'the idea' to change the way safety worked, it was a tech idea, which of course Big Sam had no idea about. He had rough concepts of what he wanted, but it was more like science fiction than anything he could even begin to know about implementing. He had confided in Johnno, probably over a few beers, who was busy trying to promote his labour business and just happened to bump into a very big global customer who wanted something like 'the idea' for his behemoth of a company that killed about forty people per year of its four hundred thousand strong workforce.

At this stage the two of them turned to Douglas. They presented it like they were doing him a favour but the truth is without him 'the idea' would have died at that moment.

Douglas, along with the help of Kit, an employee of Douglas' tech support company had completed the early technical concept, filling in Sam's science fiction with facts of what could be achieved. Douglas had then used Kit and another of his staff, Jimmy, to develop a real prototype, something you could hold in your hand that, mostly, worked. Douglas and Kit had worked with OV, short for Octavius Verwemm, a local patent guru and some US lawyers to develop the patent. Douglas and Kit had even delivered some early wins on certification. To that point Sam hadn't even contributed any money, Douglas was ready to pack it in and then finally Sam agreed to stump up the business, mostly with money from previous business associates.

So the venture was born.

The original agreement was that he was going to be technical, he didn't really want to be the CEO, but it was like one of those reverse volunteer lines. Douglas just stood still while Sam took a step back. The same was true when Johnno came in, he paid a very small amount of money for shares and appeared at board meetings, but he did very little without Douglas being leaned on to complete the necessary task at hand.

Douglas had been approached to sell his own company, as had Sam, and the two entered negotiations figuring they could work on the new venture together, but that's not how it worked out. Sam got golden handcuffs for two years, keeping him fully engaged in his old company on a huge retainer, while Douglas was left running the new venture on his own.

So it was Douglas' show. Now he wasn't well, he saw Sam and Johnno actually didn't really care that a friend was sick, they just cared that someone they had relied on couldn't be relied on anymore. Maybe they thought he was faking it.

Why would he do that? He built it.

The whole Amber thing had muddied the waters, both Sam and Johnno knew about Amber and seemed unconcerned when Douglas was doing what they needed him to do. But now he was incapacitated and wouldn't get to it, it was his fault for playing around with a younger woman.

These thoughts had spun in Douglas' head for months, now and probably would for the rest of his life.

If she hadn't walked in.

That day still burned in his mind. She had on shin high leather boots, leather accessories that looked like they were destined for a nightclub. A business shirt and trousers with a jacket which looked like she had inherited from one of the members of Duran Duran. It was a great look and she pulled it off perfectly. Just the right amount of scent added so she felt good but didn't over power anyone who got too close.

Douglas thought they had developed a special bond before the interview was over. Like most interviews at that early stage it was just him, unless it was a tech interview and then it was Paul as well. Douglas was sure Paul would not approve, just on looks alone, but he hired Amber anyway, she certainly had the experience.

Douglas was never in a million years thinking she would be slightly interested in him, and then she was. What a surprise that was. From the other side of the office Douglas and Amber shared with Paul she crossed and embraced him. Not in a friendly coworker way, but in an emotionally suggestive, almost loving way.

The two of them had spent plenty of time alone together. Douglas was not a stay in the office type of guy. They had gone for coffee and lunch and drinks. Truth is he had done the same with Paul and even with Kit sometimes, although Kit didn't drink and didn't like coffee so that was limited.

The first trip away together was almost magical to Douglas, even if he didn't see it until they came back. It must have also been to Amber. Without him noticing, she had been seeing him either for what he was now or at least the remnants of what he had been. More thoughts that would spin in his head forever. His head hurt when he thought about Amber and the venture, Big Sam, the idea, the customer, Johnno and the whole thing. His head hurt and it spread through his body until the fibre in his bones cried out.

Douglas sighed deeply and drifted into a trouble sleep. One day these things would pass and he would reach out to take the chance to move on when it came.

What, if anything, would they all say about him and would it really matter to him then?

***

Will moved slowly so he could look in the window of the old brick building.

He had studied all the online maps and tourist sites to find where other pubs similar to the white house were, both around the old harbour and surrounding areas. He figured Ruud might head to a different location but he is going to hang out in similar places. Will just couldn't see Ruud operating out of a coffee shop, a five star hotel lobby or a lock up. Ruud was a pub guy. Unfortunately there were a lot of pubs.

On his first count Will found eighty pubs on the map, but while he was scoping out the first five he found another two that weren't on any maps. Those were the most likely candidates for Ruud to be in, something only locals knew about. The fact was that Ruud probably operated out of more than one, maybe even several at a time.

He didn't dally long as worse than not finding Ruud would be finding him and Ruud seeing Will. Worse still would be Ruud seeing Will looking for Ruud and Will not seeing Ruud. Will was hoping to trail Ruud or Goos or Kobus if he could find any of them and get a better idea of where they hung out and what they actually did.

Will had taken a leaf out of Eugene's book and was working through it logically, his thoughts were to work on a grid, moving out from the white house. It may have just been coincidence that they were in the white house that day or it might be a pattern that they follow.

No luck, so Will moved on. He did remember that most meetings were at lunch time so he would go out everyday around that time. It was also possible they had headed out of Rotterdam for a while to lay low, but ten thousand Euro's split three ways wouldn't really be enough to do much, so chances are they were close by and this was their patch so they knew the lay of the land very very well.

Will tried another three bars and after fortuitously spotting a car park outside a coffee shop stopped to go inside, just for a coffee. Since staying at Eugene's place he had not taken in anything illicit, just had alcohol to drink, just had that one ecstacy tab in Club Blu and nothing to smoke. It seemed better to stick by Eugene's rules especially when he was paying for all the booze. But here he was in Holland, it would be a terrible shame not to have a smoke, legally for a change.

Will sat quietly looking out the window at a park diagonally up the street. He craned his head to get a better view before relaxing as the contents of the joint eased the tension in his muscles with a slow drawn out effect.

If he didn't find Ruud, how was he going to broach the subject with Eugene on the missing money. He didn't come here to rip off his friend. Of all the shady deals he had previously been a part of, this stuck in his throat a lot. He could count his true friends on one hand.

He sighed and tried to lose his thoughts in the swaying of the small trees on the edge of the park.

In what he could only see as an act of fate, who should walk out of the park but Goos. He turned and walked the opposite way to which Will was, but it was unmistakably him. Will took a final mouthful of his coffee and walked out as quickly as possible following Goos at a distance. Will wasn't used to tailing someone and after a few hundred meters he realised he had lost him. Still, his thoughts were correct, they didn't go far.

Will now had an area to focus on and it wasn't far from where he thought.

***

Will hadn't returned to the coffee shop but took an hour to sit in the park while the THC passed through his body. From the park it was a short walk to the dream bakery and he found Eugene in the kitchen making a sandwich.

"I honestly wasn't sure you had food here," Will quipped, grinning.

"It's a kitchen," Eugene replied with stupid look on his face.

"Suppose I could get one?" Will wasn't hungry before he saw the food but that had quickly changed.

"Everything is at your disposal," Eugene said in a grandiose tone. "Baked goods, dairy, condiments, fresh ingredients, utensils" he tapped each cupboard or drawer as he listed off the items needed to make a sandwich.

"Vegemite?" Will inquired like a puppy pleading for a treat.

"Indeed," Eugene opened a drawer and bought out a large jar of the Australian yeast extract food spread.

Will brushed passed Eugene and made himself two large Vegemite sandwiches. He hadn't had Vegemite since he left Australia. The salty taste left him with memories of his childhood, one of the rare good memories.

"So," Eugene broke in. "I made some changes to the shielding in the dream interceptor and lowered some of the power ratios to further minimise electromagnetic radiation."

Eugene shuffled slightly.

"Think it's enough?" Will asked.

"Daaisi also found a few modifications to the seed function to specifically lead the dreamer away from random animal images."

"How does that work?" Will said, immediately regretting his question.

"The seeding is hierarchical, with a theoretical matrix of possibilities that can be achieved if a variation of sound and image is seen and accepted by the mind. By removing the animals and subsequent associated images from the hierarchy it should preclude the dreamer from reaching the thought of animals in general." Eugene's explanation was delivered with his usual confidence.

"Sound's like a very unproven theory." Will noted, "same could be said in reverse, that you are better to include the animal in, and all its subsequent associated images modifying them to make them friendly." He smiled, mocking Eugene slightly,

"Indeed." Eugene clearly didn't see that he was being mocked. Will knew that he was grasping and he had absolutely no idea where totems came from.

"I suppose you are going to ask me to take it for a test drive for you." Will aimed a serious look at Eugene raising one eyebrow slightly to signify his disdain.

"No no, not at all," Eugene added.

"Good, because I'm just not, still not quite over my close encounter with Squidward." Will changed his face to show his bruised pride.

"Just thought you would like to know," Eugene replied. "I have one of my test subjects coming around tomorrow. She saw a Beaver last time so I am hoping there is no more of that."

"So not everyone gets one of these animals?" Will asked.

"Including you we have five out of two hundred and fifty odd test subjects." Eugene shrugged, "I have gone over the test data and just can't seem to gather what its all about. If I reduce it to people who have been tested multiple times it is more like five out of fifty. Ten percent."

"Still," Will replied. "Are you confident the changes you made will stop the demons coming to he surface? Tell me at least you have done enough to remove the risk of physical harm."

"Oh yes," Eugene added. "I also put in an emergency shut down element which will remove all power to the dream interceptor when the subject shows any ill effects. From there I have added an emergency protocol to Daaisi's wake up procedures."

"Sounds like you have covered some bases," Will mocked completing his sandwich and returning to the kitchen. "Any way to make toasties?" he asked.

"Third drawer from the left has a sandwich press, cheese in the fridge if you want Vegemite and cheese," Eugene replied.

"Now we are talking," Will cried with glee.

***

Adrie was so happy to receive Eugene's appointment email.

Life had become tedious as she danced around the elephant in the room that now lived in the house she had built with Douglas.

She had found the Harrods bag and a number of other items of a female nature on a personal credit card that Douglas would use, purchased around eight months ago. She had no doubt now, but was unable to get any more information on who it might possibly be. Maybe someone Douglas worked with, or one of the customers he was always visiting. She didn't know anyone associated with his work except Sam and Johnno and that nice man Paul and young Kit, of course. She just couldn't imagine asking them and she had never been to the Rotterdam office and wouldn't even know where the office in London was. So it all seemed pointless.

She was ready to confront him before the email arrived, so now she would have one more try and then, maybe, if she was lucky she would have the last part of the puzzle. Before the session had started Eugene told her he had worked out a series of seed images just for her. First to try and remove the beaver and any associated images from her dream. He said this was fairly new, as he had been mostly interested in putting images into peoples dreams and controlling a narrative. He kept the concept the same thinking that by removing things that might appear he might similarly control them.

Now after the session, Adrie sat quietly in the kitchen chair waiting patiently for her coffee.

Her hand shook slightly like she was a marionette with strings that were being danced on. Her eyes didn't focus on Eugene but seemed to vaguely find a spot in the corner of the room before darting to another and then at an equally random interval, another. Her decline was very evident and only her fourth visit.

Eugene placed the coffee in front of her, looking at her intently. It took her a few seconds for her to focus and return her gaze his way.

"Thanks pet. Oh what lovely green eyes you have."

"You're welcome. Thanks." Eugene said unsure which was the better reply. "Everything okay?"

"Bit wonky, but I am sure this will fix it" she added holding up the coffee cup.

The two sat quietly, Adrie could seem to find the right words and hardly noticed how worried her host had become.

***

Paige struggled to raise her head. Life was now movement in molasses again. Her arms felt heavy and her legs dragged like they were tethered to rails.

What had happened?

Her mental state had degraded so quickly in the days since Charlotte had moved out. If she was honest with herself her thoughts had been headed that way since before that day. It wasn't an overnight thing, it was like a cycle, an enigmatic glutinous rotation making her torpid brain languorous and feeble.

She just needed to crawl into bed and wait it out. Charlotte only came to visit twice in the two weeks since she moved out. Both times, it appeared to be just for sex, she didn't sleep over and didn't stay long and the conversation was just pleasantries until it wasn't conversation anymore. Then she was gone.

Lying in bed, underneath her covers, cold and alone Paige started to feel very much like she had when she was with Eugene. Not when Eugene was around, just when he wasn't around or had locked himself in his study area. Actually, she concluded, when Eugene was around she rarely felt this way. His presence had lifted her out of this a lot, better than with any other partner or lover she had before or since, certainly way more than with Charlotte.

She thought back on how much he had tried to break her out of these times, sometime to his own detriment and his own mental anguish. He listened so carefully to her babble, piecing together her inane nonsense and not just recounting it back, but organising it and making some semblance of sense of it. He had even tried to lift her up out of it and show her how she could turn the malaise into action, in her own time.

Paige tried hard to remember why she left. It was the boy, she was sure, he would shout 'get out' and 'run' in her dreams. But was that from Eugene? Now she thought back it really wasn't really very clear.

Paige cried for a while. What had she done, what an idiot. It had been such a bad year.

How would she even start to make contact now that so much time had passed?

She had seen so many people since she had been back in London trying so hard to wash away his memory, but there it was so clear and so bright.

Chapter Nine

The Finality of Realisation

Adrie looked good in black.

She had a number of black outfits. Most were to accentuate her curves, to excite those who looked and foremost in her mind to keep the interest of Douglas.

Black was a colour that showed up her skin tone the best. Classic Nordic white. Black was also a perfect colour to accessorise with. Red's to catch fire, colourful gems and stones to glitter and gold to shine.

Adrie liked to wear black. But on this occasion it had little meaning.

Sass had helped her to dress, quietly, without changing, she accepted the formal outfit that Sass had chosen. She had slipped on her most unattractive but comfortable black shoes and rejected everything but the watch that Douglas had bought her for her fortieth birthday. Her interest in appearance had to take a back seat today. No makeup, no perfume, just her, as she would let only Douglas see her.

The car pulled up outside the house. Sass held her arm as she walked out the door and deposited her into the cool leather of the back seat. Like a cue to begin, the rain cried a slow crawl, more like a Rotterdam mist, devoid of wind. Adrie knew that today she would join the sky and mourn openly but for now she held back and instead squeezed hard on Sass' hand as she took her place beside Adrie in the back seat.

The funeral home was only a short ride but within her mind Adrie spanned a life time. She focused on the good times with Douglas, his chivalrous side, his genius, his quick wit and his unique way of looking at the world. He was an irreplaceable part of her life that she now tried to capture and hold in her memory.

The driver pulled into the destination and delivered Adrie to the main entrance. It was covered and had a small group of ladies standing waiting. They waited for her, to embrace her and to care for her and to share her grief as they had shared her life. They all knew Douglas, they would all miss Douglas.

This brief respite from the truth at hand was interrupted by an usher from the funeral home who ferried Adrie alone into a small room to the side where she was given a series of instructions. Most of the words the usher said bounced around in her mind before she gave a resigned acceptance and acknowledgement. Like a final act to confirm that Douglas was indeed passed from this life.

With his tasks accomplished the usher left the room, leaving Adrie alone. She waited for a few moments accepting she needed to get used to this feeling.

Sass entered from the small door and grabbed her hand. "It's time my beauty," she said solemnly.

Adrie was shown to a seat in the front. The hall wasn't full but there was a good showing of people. Douglas was not popular, she would almost say he didn't have many friends. But he was always friendly and eager to participate if asked. Especially in his younger years. She didn't see it then but now she realised he had given a lot of that up to work, to work for the things she and others took for granted. Did he work because he enjoyed what he did or was he resigned to his place in the world.

She never asked and now she would never know.

Paul gave a beautiful speech. Eulogising Douglas' majestic grasp on technology and industry and in his early days on a pint of Guinness. Kriall spoke from the heart of Douglas' songwriting and how the music community of the past appreciated his energy and his attempt to trail blaze fusing different styles, those of his making and other styles without a name yet.

Finally it was down to Adrie. She had let her tears fall openly through the service and with support from Sass and Juul had remained in touch with the service through the fog of her own internal grief. Sass stood to give her support as she made her way to the dias but she touched her friends arm and asked her to sit. She would do this alone.

Standing alone in her weakness she read.

"A eulogy for Douglas by Douglas

The sunshine plays on the dust and so I will return to dust

The raindrops bounce in the dust and so I will return to dust

The wheat grows in the dust and so I will return to dust

The lamb walks on the dust and so I will return to dust

The house I call home is but dust and so I will return to dust

You breathe in the dust and so I will return to dust

The world that turns came from dust and so I will return to that dust

Death is now for the living to contend with, as now my body goes to dust"

Douglas was explicit that there would be no God in anything to do with his passing and so left little comfort for Adrie that she couldn't extract from her friends.

Many people milled around her after the service. But Adrie was numb and while she remembered the discussions and the feelings, for the life of her she couldn't recall the content. Her friends were beautiful and gave her comfort at every step. Sass ensured she got home safely and stayed with her for a few days before her own life beckoned and required her to return. Fleur had stepped in during day times and Janna stayed with her a few nights as the first week and then the second passed. Eventually though, they all had lives and while they were always on the end of the phone Adrie's big home became bigger as she was left to fend for herself.

The afternoon was dreary outside some weeks later, but it was of slight regard to Adrie who had accumulated a colourless afternoon indoors. She couldn't bear to reminisce further and instead had reduced herself to watching daytime soap opera on TV.

The lead actor had just admitted to his wife of his extramarital affair with a lady from his office when Douglas' phone rang. Adrie hadn't cut it off yet, it had a rung a few times and she thought it best to keep it going to let people know Douglas had passed. She fully expected Big Sam or Johnno to come looking for it but they didn't and she wasn't ready to give Douglas' things away just yet.

"Good Afternoon Madam. This is Brent Stuart from the Clear Sky Apartments in London. Looking for Douglas Winters."

"Yes, hello Brent. This is his wife or should I say widow. I am sorry to say that Douglas passed away recently." Adrie took a breath. It was still quite a surreal thing for her to say.

"Oh, sorry for your loss. That would explain a lot."

"Can I help," Adrie replied curiously.

"Yes. Douglas had a long term apartment rented here at The Clear Sky. We noticed that he hadn't been here for over a month and generally he paid one month in advance but we didn't receive payment so I thought I would give a quick call. The apartment also has some personal effects inside."

"Oh yes" Adrie replied, she knew he had somewhere and so finally this was it. "I apologise, I meant to travel over to clear things up, you know, just a bit lacking motivation. If I give you a credit card will that help with the money side. Maybe keep the place the way it is for the moment. I can be there tomorrow to clean out the personal effects. Is that OK pet?"

"No problems, Mrs Winters, please when you come tomorrow ask for me, Mr Stuart and I will let you in and we can discuss things face to face."

"Perfect, I appreciate your understanding Mr Stuart I will see you around midday."

The following day Adrie took the train down to Brussels and then across to smelly old London. She had never liked London much, great shopping but the overall city was so overwhelming, depressing and aggravating all at once. She would much prefer to go to Amsterdam or Dusseldorf or Bremen, they all had charm. London, Paris and Frankfurt had become big dirty cesspits of the world. She was sure once they were all great cities but the full drawbacks of mass immigration could been seen in its full splendour now. They were not so much the melting pots of the world as the collection of the ugliest people of all cultures all holed up in little gang territories trying to hold on to what they had left behind grasping for money, gasping for air.

Adrie didn't plan to stay the night. She had left early, hoping to see Mr Stuart before noon, clean up Douglas stuff quickly and be back in Rotterdam before nightfall.

Mr Stuart was very lovely. He made her a quick cup of instant coffee and sat her down in his office. After he ensured she wasn't going to burst out in tears on him he was also very thorough, checking Adrie's identification and then presenting her an invoice and finalising her new credit details before presenting her a key. He escorted her to the apartment and asked if she would like him to come in or if she would prefer some time alone.

Adrie decided alone would be better and so Mr Stuart took his leave.

Her entry was profound. As she suspected, it was the apartment from her dream photograph. She took a moment to absorb how amazing that Dream Photographer was. She had never seen this place and yet his re-creation was almost perfect. She sat down at the small desk and fumbled amongst a few of Douglas' things. The pen was one she had bought him, the notebook brimming with calculations, sketches, tables and diagrams. She would need to get that to Paul. In the cupboard were a variety of shirts, trousers and jackets. She bought them up to her face one by one searching for a hint of Douglas' but they just smelled like dry cleaning and hotel cupboard.

She moved to the bedroom, the bed was made and clean. On the offending bedside table there was nothing, on the shelf by the office nothing. If there was someone else living here they had vacated and taken with them everything.

Adrie thought for a moment if it even mattered anymore. Douglas was gone.

She took a moment to gather her energy for the task ahead. She collected everything up and put in the suitcase she found in the cupboard. She was prepared with a big bag but the suitcase was easier.

As she left she saw a cleaner outside, she took a moment to say hello and ask if the cleaner knew Douglas. The cleaner did recall him and his daughter who visited with him.

"Daughter?" Adrie asked.

"Yes," the cleaner said, "pretty little thing. They did look a bit a like. I assumed he was her father."

Adrie packed up and headed back to Rotterdam, making it home before night fall.

With a large glass of wine in hand she looked at the collection of Douglas' work things. There was nothing in there about a pretty young thing, she couldn't even find a recent staff list. She thought the whole company was made up of nerdy boys. Maybe she could ask Paul. How would she do that though without raising suspicion.

Adrie turned over the documents again and instead turned her attention to Douglas tablet and phone. No pictures or messages but in an inspired moment Adrie had a quick check of the recycle bin on Douglas' phone.

She didn't have to scroll far to find some old messages he had sent to a number with no name and only one reply.

"I'm OK and back in Rotterdam"

"Good to hear. Back to your wife. Probably for the best."

"Give me some time to get better and I will be back in London."

"Don't go cold on me baby."

"Please."

The last text seemed a little desperate for Douglas.

Adrie thought for a very short moment and then called that number from Douglas' phone. She got increasingly more agitated as the phone rang and even more so as after five rings it just cut out. No pickup, no voicemail.

Adrie called again and repeated her action three times before throwing the phone into the box.

She needed to find out who the other woman is.

***

121

Will had spent a few weeks now scouting around the area where he had first glimpsed Goos coming out of the park. Truth be told he had spent a lot of that time getting baked in the coffee shop. The weed was particularly mellow. Eugene was locked away in his study, so he had to do something.

It was one such day when finally Goos came out of the same park.

This time, even though he was a little under the affects of the soft gentle weed he managed to follow Goos a little better. He tracked him to a small local bar, very well hidden down a small alleyway. Will was very sure this was not on any map and was a little unsure it was even a public bar. It looked like one of those ethnic hangouts, devoid of advertising or signage with very rudimentary furniture and often with some very sullen looking character in the front running crowd control.

It had Ruud written all over it.

Standing on the street, Will stood out badly, so didn't stop long. He cased the area and quickly made his way into a shop on the street opposite which would hopefully give him a good view of the alley. The shop was one of those new fashion stores with just the name in bold writing on the front and a negligible display window. Actually the window just had a single suggestive outfit in it, black leather which only just covered up the critical areas.

Opening the door Will was a little caught by the music which was heavy, almost industrial, he turned into the shop and it all became clear. The shop assistant came from out of a backroom and not to be fazed Will turned and started to browse some pegging outfits.

"Anything I can help with," the assistant cried out, "just let me know."

"Thanks Hun." Will replied. "Just having a look for now."

Will tried to stay around the front so he could get a view of the alley way.

He worked his way along hangers at the front which were all pegging apparatus. Will was astounded. He was a man of the world but he had no concept there were so many different types of outfits for that particular entanglement.

"Are you Australian?"

Will didn't so much jump and took a double take. The shop assistant, who he could see now was a tall woman as only dutch women can be, had silently made her way up behind him while he was looking out the window and fondling a large leather belt.

"Yeah, from the land 'Down Under'" he accentuated the accent as many Australian's do. People seemed to like it.

"Oh that's so darling." The shop assistant had an angular face that at first look seemed kind and harsh all at the same time. Will moved along the rack a little.

"This one gives better stability sweetie, grips better at the hips. You don't want anyone slipping on the thrust."

"Certainly don't." Will was not embarrassed, just well out of his depth.

"What brings you to Rotterdam my little Kangaroo." The shop assistant said, genuinely trying to be friendly.

"Just catching up with a friend who lives here."

"Ah OK, that's nice. Is she in the bar over there?" The shop assistant added.

"Huh, no, ah maybe, not sure." Will stammered over his words.

"Good to hear, that's not a nice place over there. I can introduce you to some nicer places if you are new here." She looked at him with an air of expectation, hoping her invitation might bare fruit.

"That sounds lovely," Will replied. "I'm Will" he added extending his hand.

"Exciting. I'm Dahlia," she replied. "How long have you been in Rotterdam?"

"A few weeks," Will replied.

"Did you have a chance to see much of the nightlife yet?"

"Just Club Blu. Mostly I have been catching up with my friend. We went to school together, but he doesn't get out much."

"Club Blu is a little tame for my liking, but lots of wildlife there. Like to scale up?" Dahlia said putting on her best suggestive face. "You can bring your friend. Is he Dutch or Australian?"

"He lives here, but he is Australian," Will replied.

"Well. I am thinking you don't want any of these but here is my number, so please send me your number and I will send you some great places to go."

Will turned and took the card but when he turned back he saw Goos come out of the bar.

"Lovely to meet you Dahlia, I will message you later maybe we can meet up, I'm good tonight if that timing works." Will was never one to miss an opportunity to go out on the town.

"Bye sweet thing. Don't be good, be safe," she smiled.

'Beautiful smile,' Will thought to himself before turning his attention back to Goos.

He followed Goos about five hundred meters up the road before Goos stopped in at a small convenience store. Will held back, not wanting to get too close or alert Goos to his presence. After about five minutes, Goos came out with a can of coke and moved along the street a little further. Then inexplicably he turned around and walked straight towards Will.

Will looked around quickly but there was no where to go, so he just acted casually.

"Goos, buddy. Fancy seeing you here. How's things?" He said casually.

"Good," Goos replied.

"Did you find anything nice?" He asked.

"Nice?" Will replied quizzically.

"In the bondage shop. Each to their own." Goos added subtly.

"Yeah, right." Will was not getting into that.

"So I was looking for you guys. Ruud around?" Will thought he was best to get straight to the point.

He didn't see the first blow, so that one hurt him the most.

Having said that the flurry of punches that Kobus let loose all hurt.

Goos just stood back and let Kobus go to work and Will had no time to do anything but curl up in a ball and protect his vital organs. Kobus was an animal and when his brief attack was over he leaned down and said to Will.

"Stay away, get out of Rotterdam. If I see you again I will kill you."

Will couldn't see but he was briefly aware that both Goos and Kobus had turned and walked away. It was mid afternoon, but in this part of Rotterdam there were not many people on the street.

Still on the ground Will moved in and out of consciousness. His ribs burned every time he breathed. Slowly he dragged himself up and moved over to the nearest house and leaned on the fence. He swooned for a few minutes before finally holding himself up without the aid of the fence.

He couldn't see Goos or Kobus but he was fairly sure they went in the direction of the convenience store so Will went the opposite way, back towards the bar. He made it about one hundred meters before collapsing again.

"Shit," he exhaled.

Will reached into his jacket. He could feel some blood on his rib cage but wasn't sure where it was from. He secured his mobile phone and called Eugene. It went to voicemail.

"Genie. I got taken down, pretty bad. Outside De Barones on Boergoensestraat if you can get here."

He didn't get a chance to finish before he blacked out again and fell on the footpath, slumped up against the fence. Will came to a few minutes after and tried Eugene again. This time he didn't leave a message. He looked up and saw the bondage store. He was loath to do it but Dahlia seemed like she would be able to take it. He got to his feet managed to walk a few paces and collapsed again. In a lucid moment her managed to get Dahlia's card out of his pocket and with his phone still in his hand he called the number..

"Dahlia," her answer was like her, straight to the point.

"This is Will, kangaroo. I didn't make it far."

"Baby that's a fast reply. I didn't expect to hear from you until at least tonight," she said jokingly.

"Yeah," Will said letting out a big coughing fit. "Sorry to drop this on you, I am about a hundred meters from your store. I got jumped when I left."

"Jumped? In broad daylight. What!?" Dahlia came out of the store and rushed towards Will.

Will was still slumped against the fence. He tried to smile but it hurt so he returned to the grimace he had been holding since the altercation.

"What happened. Are they still around?"

"Gone," Will needed to minimise his words. His lungs were on fire and that was indeed blood coming from under his jacket.

"Can we go to your store?"

"Sure," she said, "Let me help you."

The two shuffled the short distance to the bondage shop. Will could feel his phone ringing in his pocket but was not in a position to answer just yet. Dahlia was not just tall, she was strong and built. She had no problem moving Will into place on a bench in the middle of the store. At first Will sat but he needed to lie flat and Dahlia could see that, so she lay him out on the bench.

"Sweets you are bleeding. You need to go to a hospital. Let me call and ambulance."

"Yeah Na," Will said using an Australian anachronism. "phone in my jacket. Eugene just called. He will get me. Can you..."

Will slipped back out of consciousness as the blood rushed from his brain to try and feed his injuries. Lucky for him Dahlia got the gist of what he needed. Next thing he saw was Eugene standing over him.

"That was quick," he quipped.

"I heard your message and was in the car calling. Dahlia here was nice enough to pick up and fill in the precise details."

"I just didn't realise there were so many of you cute kangaroo's floating around in my little town," she said smiling. "This little one needs a hospital" she added, changing her facial expression to one of concern.

"He does," Eugene agreed. "No choice buddy. Trust me."

"Yep. Lets try and keep the cops out if we can."

"Do you mind to help me get him to the car." Eugene said to Dahlia

"Of course," she said.

***

Eugene pulled his Audi into the car park which was part of the rear of the dream bakery. The roller doors formed what looked like a wall outside. It would have been difficult to know it was a garage if you ignored the concrete driveway.

Will looked much better. Amazing what a few days in hospital will do.

His ribs were broken but any complications that had come from the injury had healed well.

Will had given the police a description of the assailants and they had some video footage. Turned out both Goos and Kobus were well known to local police. The only point of query was around the conversation Will had with the shifty looking guy before the big guy handed out his beating.

Will said they just wanted him to give them money. The footage pretty much confirmed that could be so, allowing police to put the whole thing down to a daylight robbery with Will just the victim. Will added he thought it was drug related. The biggest blessing was Dahlia's corroboration of the lead up and of the known drug activity in the area, particularly in the alley across the road.

Now off the hook Will thought it was best to come clean with Eugene.

The two shared a coffee in the kitchen followed by a heart to heart about what Will had been up to and where the money Eugene had loaned him had gone. Will knew it could mean the end of the friendship but he also knew it would be worse if he lied about anything at this point.

Eugene was not really worried. Ten thousand Euro's was nothing to sneeze at, but his accumulated wealth dwarfed that number and he had a way to make money on demand if he needed it. Not legally, but he had a way. Eugene's major

127

concern was to ascertain that Will wasn't taking advantage of him. He cross examined his friend carefully and watched hard to gauge his body language and mannerisms. The two talked for a few hours, ate a meal together, laughed a little and talked some more. Eugene could see no evidence that Will was anything but his friend, so he let it go.

It was as easy a conversation as it usually was, unique as it came without alcohol lubricating the rough edges but still thoroughly enjoyed by both.

Chapter Ten

Domino's can't defy gravity

Adrie was on time and this time Eugene met her at the door.

She had responded immediately to his email confirming an appointment, after her request to uncover the identity of the person in her dream making love to her husband. She had told Eugene she had seen to room from the dream photograph and was convinced that if she could dream up the room, she could dream up the girl.

Eugene had worked out a very specific image and sound seed, based on further information Adrie had provided about the room. It allowed Eugene to work out the angles and adjust the information to rotate the picture. That's how things had worked out with Lem and he had done such things in his own dreams and Paige's.

Eugene was nervous, he had made a few further adjustments to the dream interceptor. He had retracted some of the wires to decrease the EMF produced and added some specialised shielding from ear pods to deflect the waves into a cavity he had placed on top of the dream interceptor. The cavity now was really just a wall of sensors but he hoped by diverting any interference away from the brain he would better control EMF.

If it was the problem.

His bench testing had shown a reduction in EMF by over fifty percent on the previous model and almost ninety percent on the original. In the original he had no concept that radiation was so high or that it might be causing a fluctuation in dream patterns. If he was honest with himself, he still wasn't sure.

Eugene had added more personal sensors to ensure better monitoring of Adrie's wellbeing during the session. He had personally modified the emergency code and had Daaisi double check. Daaisi had been researching a wide variety of shutdown and emergency codes from medical scenario's and from industry. Places where if you don't act fast, people die.

The last two weeks had all been about this moment and while he was not confident, he knew the only way forward was trial and error.

"So just to be clear, I need your consent again," Eugene said.

"Of course pet," Adrie replied. She was very keen.

"The AI is going to outline some legalities at the end just say 'I consent'," Eugene explained.

"Some bits of it have changed in line with the changes to the tech and to the procedure."

"OK pet," Adrie smiled at Eugene.

"I have put new safeguards in ..." Eugene began.

Adrie raised her hand.

"I trust you," she said.

Eugene's heart fell. He didn't want her trust, he wanted her to understand.

"I will be watching from the kitchen. Any sign of trouble and distress I will be ending the session. I don't want to take any chances."

"Great," Adrie replied.

'Let's find this bitch.'

She wanted to say it but Adrie just thought it instead.

"See you on the other side for coffee," he said touching her arm in a comforting gesture.

By the time Eugene reached the kitchen Adrie was lying down on the day bed, watching the images he had produced. The images were not difficult to find, order and present but the sounds were a little more difficult. Eugene had settled on some Elgar Cello music, the noise of an elevator, wind from the top of a building, a shower running and the white noise that you often get in well soundproofed rooms.

Adrie's heart rate slowly dropped as she lingered around consciousness before she entered a good non-rapid eye movement (NREM) sleep. Eugene watched her vital signs all of which were normal and well within parameters he had set specifically for Adrie based on her previous visits. In particular her first visit which went without any issues. He considered this the baseline and was going to be intolerant of any deviation. Adrie moved resolutely through NREM phase one and two. Her body temperature fell slightly as she clung to phase two marginally longer than her first visit but only just before reaching the deeper sleep attributed to phase three NREM sleep.

An hour had passed and Eugene had not moved position, he thought it wise to get some water so moved to the fridge and retrieved a bottle of still Evian.

Adrie drifted slightly, her body now at its lowest ebb ready and waiting for REM sleep to start. Her brain activity exploded into action. Eugene studied the graphs intently looking for any anomaly, the blue line of the current sessions matched so clearly against the yellow line of the first session. So tightly matched it was almost a repeat.

Then it wasn't. Ten minutes had gone by, her dream seemed to be ready to conclude when a huge spike in brain activity led to a major change in her physiology. In a second her blood pressure increased and her brain activity centred on a single area before closing down completely.

Daaisi had shutdown the session within that second.

Eugene waited a moment trying to comprehend what had just happened. All the EMF sensors showed no change, room diagnostics on power, temperature, humidity all nothing. Adrie's own physical attributes showed normal and then spiked particularly in one area.

"Not good," Eugene pondered and immediately changed his focus to Adrie.

He rushed into the interview room to see Adrie still lying on the bed. Eugene reached for her forearm and took her pulse.

She still had a heartbeat. Small miracles.

"Medical Report," he called out as a signal to Daaisi that he needed information.

"The heart rate and blood pressure of Subject 260 are returning to normal but body temperature is dangerously low. Compensating room temperature but this is likely to be ineffectual in the short term. Medical recommendations are to administer saline based fluids but as the Subject 260 is unconscious this will need to be via an intravenous drip."

Eugene had a full medical kit in the hall outside between the two interview rooms.

He made his way quickly to the medical cupboard. It was immaculately organised now with an AED defibrillator, vital signs monitors, a spirometer and other measuring devices, and a large trauma kit. Eugene also had arranged a large collection of common medicines, antihistamines and anti-inflammatory drugs. He couldn't immediately see an I.V. drip so opened the trauma kit before remembering he had itemised the contents.

"Is there an I.V. drip in Medical Store One," he barked out loud.

"No Eugene,"

Eugene swore allowed.

"Problems mate," Will said from the doorway of interview room two.

"Big problems," Eugene replied. "I would say fairly catastrophic." The look on his face was an open book and Will responded quickly.

Will followed Eugene into the interview room and saw Adrie, unconscious.

"I am assuming she's alive," he said. "She looks bad, we should take her to a hospital ASAP."

"Agreed," said Eugene with an air of resignation. "There are consequences, but lets worry about those later."

The two of them gently lifted Adrie and moved her down the hall to the car park slipping her into a lying down position on the back seat of Eugene's Audi.

"I have to do something a little strange before we go," Eugene said looking at Will intently.

"Sure mate, what do I need to do," Will said gingerly. His lungs had almost recovered but if you asked the doctor about lifting people he would have said to avoid that particular activity.

"Can you start the car and put the heater on 25C. She is cold and likely to get colder if we don't warm her up." Eugene said sternly.

"I'll quickly grab my blanket too," Will said, dashing back down the hall.

"and some hoodies," Eugene called out.

Eugene lifted up the rear luggage compartment door and retrieved some tools from the back. With a quick motion he wrenched off the number plate cover to expose the screws that fastened the number plate. He removed the back license plate quickly and tossed it to the side of the car park area.

Will returned with a large woollen blanket and some hoodies as Eugene started his work on the front license plate.

"We going in anonymously," Will smiled.

"Drop and run I think," Eugene wasn't smiling.

"Right, lets do this," Will was well versed in the less salubrious side of the law.

Will rugged Adrie up as best he could. The hospital was about ten minutes away. Eugene drove very steady so as not to attract any more attention than was necessary, given he had no plates. They drove up to the emergency door and dressed in a grey hoodie Will got out and grabbed a nearby wheelchair. Eugene, dressed in a black hoodie, gently guided Adrie to the edge of the car and the two placed Adrie in the chair. Eugene returned to the drivers seat just as two orderlies came out.

"You can't stop there," one of them said.

"Just dropping off," Will said turning to return to the car. "Her details are in the bag."

His words trailed off as Eugene moved the car away. He did so fast but so as not to attract the attention of any security around the area.

"Is that an offence here?" Will asked.

"Not sure," Eugene replied. "Daaisi, is is illegal in the Netherlands to anonymously take a patient to hospital and leave them in the care of the staff."

"She is in the car too?" Will said with a dumb surprised look on his face.

"Everywhere," Eugene replied holding up his mobile phone. "Sat phone too."

"Admitting a patient anonymously is not a criminal offence in the Netherlands however it is likely to be the subject of further investigation if it is thought to be the result of criminal activity." Daaisi responded succinctly.

"Like if two dodgy blokes in hoodies do a drop off in a black Audi with no plates." Will guffawed.

"Don't answer that," Eugene gave Will an unimpressed look.

"So this is not going to go well but I suspect we have some time," Eugene said to Will.

"Right, where are you going?" Will asked.

"Just taking a few extra corners. There are some parts of Rotterdam that have less camera's than others. Some camera's recently broken, especially leading into the back of the dream bakery"

"Right," Will had completely underestimated his friends penchant for the illegal.

Eugene parked the Audi and the two made there way back to the kitchen.

"Few things I need to go through," Eugene said. "My turn to come clean."

Will looked worried.

"Bit early but I suspect we might be needing the strong stuff." Will said opening the cupboard that held the whisky collection.

"I was thinking a coffee," Eugene said taking his place near the machine "but maybe a mix is appropriate."

"So," Eugene sighed deeply. "The guy that died, died here in just that way."

Will sat passively, he knew there was more.

"But I moved him into a park near his house and like a blessing for my actions it snowed that night."

"So that cop was onto something," Will replied.

"He was indeed and I am pretty sure he was put off or had other things to do or whatever. But now..." Eugene cut his words short.

"But now he's going to put two and two together and go hard." Will said. "That's not going to be good for either of us. As far as I know he doesn't have my name but if he gets it I will be in the shit too."

"When he does..." Eugene didn't need to finish the sentence but made an explosion sign with his right hand while his left fitted the coffee portafilter.

"Mate I am not the one with the sizeable investment here. I am a ghost not on the radar and I can be again," Will said. "Persona non grata, that's me. I can be gone in a flash."

Eugene finished up the coffee pour and moved to lengthening the milk.

"Something I have been working on," Eugene confessed.

"Really," Will said.

"I have been cleaning up a lot of the physical evidence. Most of it is now in some select lockups around Holland. Daaisi has been re-written to be 100% cloud except during operations, just for speed and then self cleaning. I also added a military grade cleanup routine so they can't extract anything from any physical equipment later. The building is owned by a company that is owned by a trust that has shareholders in Cayman Islands none of which is me. It would take them a long time to unravel that side. My money is crypto, very easy to access from anywhere and the small amount I leave here in Euros will just be a smoke screen."

Will was gobsmacked.

"So I could also be a bit of a ghost," Eugene added. "Just a little unsure of how to get around border posts. But I know some people who can help if needed."

"That's probably my bit." Will smiled. "Sounds like we are off on a boy's trip."

"I think it's prudent," Eugene resigned. "Daaisi can provide cover. Making it appear we are still here, unless they do surveillance. Still it will give us time." Eugene looked very resolutely at Will.

"I don't want to rope you into this." Eugene added delivering a beautifully constructed flat white coffee in front of Will. Will popped the cork on a Tullamore Dew Irish whisky and topped it off to start the afternoon on a better footing.

"What else am I going to do," Will said. "I can't let down a mate, plus I think I owe you."

"That is a bad reason," Eugene replied. "You don't owe me, you need to come for the first reason and with the knowledge you can exit at anytime if things get too hot or you feel there is something better for you elsewhere."

"Thanks buddy. One big question though." Will said with a serious look on his face. "Are we taking these?" He held up the bottle of Tullamore Dew and a bottle of limited edition Bushmills with a smile on his face.

"So let's talk logistics," Eugene said. "We can go via air. I have a guy who runs an airline out of a local airstrip who could get us out of the EU with a few hours notice. Small plane, limited luggage space and I would say my dream stuff takes priority over these." Eugene pointed to the two bottle of Irish Whisky.

Will put on a deliberate sad face, sipping his coffee like it was a last meal on death row. At Eugene's behest the two moved back to the garage drinks in hand.

"Or," Eugene added a dramatic pause pointing to the second car in the garage.

"We can pack up the Range Rover and go on a driving holiday. There is more than enough room for whisky, coffee machines, dream equipment and even your fancy roller suitcase. I think we have time to drive to pretty much any border post around the Black Sea or Mediterranean and then ferry with the car to wherever."

"That definitely has some merit" Will replied. "Gives us time to organise things while being on the move and means we don't have to use any agents or anyone else for a while. Technically we are just on a trip taking your fancy car for a spin."

"It has a top box," Eugene added. "I could have all the dream equipment in that leaving more than enough room for a few more of these." Eugene said pointing to the whiskey bottle Will had in his hand.

"I am liking that," Will replied.

"So about the guy that died." Will turned the conversation to a serious side. "He died in his dreams?"

"He did," Eugene replied.

"Daaisi, show Subject 259's last photo on the garage screen," Eugene called out.

He turned to Will and added with some gravitas "Extracted the detail right up until he died."

The last render of Lem's with him being gunned down in the New York street appeared on the screen.

"That's intense," Will gasped. "Gunned down in his dreams and died in real life."

"Makes no sense, but the truth is a hard detail to overlook," Eugene replied.

"So you don't have a handle on what this is," Will asked Eugene with a very serious tone.

"I don't," said Eugene," but that lady, Adrie, was on appointment number five. Lem was double that. I pushed myself well past twenty and Paige was around twenty also. Other people were generally one or two appointments."

"So it's more likely something within those people than something you do, or at least a reaction they have to what you do, that others don't react to."

"You had it after three sessions," Eugene reminded Will. "If we had continued it's likely I would be dropping you off at the park or the hospital or worse."

"Yeah, good we stopped," Will sighed. "But it would be good to know why."

"I need time to analyse the details of Adrie's incident" Eugene pondered. Already, somehow he was thinking of solutions.

"Would it help to get some info," Will added.

"Sure, what do you have in mind."

"Leave it with me."

As the two were talking Eugene received a message. The message came through to his anonymous email on his dark web account. It was the account he often used for more clandestine communications with shady people but was also the account he used to monitor communications with Paige.

He took a moment to check the contents and to his astonishment it was from Paige.

"Hi. I'm in Amsterdam tomorrow, just for the day, if you have time to meet me for lunch."

***

Will walked into the venue proudly.

He had been in places that were far worse. Some of the bars in Thailand had tabletop humping or sex shows and Will had grown up in Kings Cross, a red light suburb in Sydney, so he saw most clubs as tame by comparison. This place seemed less about sex and more about S&M, even more precisely, less S and more M. It's a generalisation, but the saying is 'it takes two'. In this case Will noticed these people seemed to be either self inflicting or being worked on by contraptions setup to inflict.

Dahlia was sitting in a booth further inside. Even amongst other tall people she stood out. Will gave the international hand signals for 'would you like a drink from the bar' and Dahlia responded by holding up her cocktail. Will settled on a beer in a bottle, something he knew he could handle and was tough to slip a mickey into. He wasn't worried about Dahlia, but the place was full of some pretty creepy clientele.

"You are looking so sweet my little Kangaroo. Don't be drinking too much as I will want to be jumping in that pouch later."

Will almost spat up his beer. Dahlia was nothing if not forward. His mind wandered to the pegging outfits.

The two had a long and lively conversation, there was no doubt in Will's mind that Dahlia bought the energy and the fun with her everywhere she went. Will bought Dahlia a second cocktail and a third. The girl seemed to have a pretty high alcohol tolerance. They talked freely about what was going on around them. Will had never actively sought out places like this, but he began to really like Dahlia and could see this was all a front for her true self.

The mirror behind them projected the central floor show. A man and a women strapped to a black metal rack. The rack was, what looked like, balanced on a pivot. As the man or woman moved, the rack would tilt one way and then the other.

Simple enough.

The game was that a small pot of wax was suspended above each rack, each pot was connected to the other persons rack so the more one person writhed in pain, or pleasure, the more wax got dripped on the second person. All of this was done to some pretty heady industrial music. Will recognised some Nine Inch Nails, some Ministry, they even played Killing Joke which was technically punk. He was loving one song but didn't know it so he ask Dahlia.

"Throbbing Gristle," she shouted.

"Amazing," Will smiled.

The two left soon after the show had finished, the end came when the couple came. It was a site to behold, a look Mum no hands kind of moment.

Dahlia had chosen a club very close to where she lived and the two had a long passionate night together. Will was not generally a spend the night kind of guy but the night seemed to go so quickly and before he knew it there was sun. That's no small feat in Rotterdam where sunrise is often quite late.

Dahlia walked out with him and the two headed for coffee and a joint at a local coffee shop.

"Do you have some magical plans for today little Kangaroo," Dahlia asked thoughtfully.

"I was going to visit a friend in hospital. Lady up the hall, she was unconscious when I checked out of the hospital. Thought I would drop in for a look."

"I am not sure you should be on the streets on your own. You can come home with me if you like or I can drop you off." She raised her eyebrows suggestively.

"I am not sure I can give or take anymore of that," Will said raising his own eyebrows, "not just now anyway. But I would appreciate a ride to the hospital. We can go in together, I have never met the lady just have a bug in me that I need to check up on her."

"Kind kangaroo too." Dahlia said with tears in her eyes. "Let's get some flowers, we can put them near her bed."

Will didn't want to go too far but this would be perfect.

The two finished their coffee's and went back towards Dahlia's. She stopped in the street beside a small light blue DAF600 and opened the door.

"This is me," she smiled, "a classic."

"This is a classic," Will admired. "Must be way older than you."

"A lady doesn't tell her age," Dahlia blushed. "It was my grandmothers car, but it still runs so well. Not that I get out much."

The two laughed and joked on the way to the hospital. When they arrived the laughs continued and it allowed Will to slip in pretty much unnoticed. He was winging it as he had no idea where Adrie was being kept or even if she was still in the hospital. He also didn't know her surname.

The two took the lift up to the ward Will was in for a few days and after a quick look at the hospital map Will realised it was that floor or the one below so it wouldn't be too hard. He just needed to keep his mouth shut in case anyone recognised the accent from the recent drop off and run.

Will strode out with confidence and stopped when he got to an empty room.

"They must have moved her." Will said looking forlorn.

"We can find her," Dahlia smiled, she was always making a game of things.

"Sounds like a plan," Will grinned. "Her first name is Adrie, but I don't know her surname."

"OK," Dahlia chuckled. "First to find her gets to choose the afternoon's activities."

"Done," said Will a little unsure where he would find the energy.

Dahlia walked back towards the floors waiting room. There were a number of families present and small collection of women all talking amongst themselves. Dahlia overheard them say the name Adrie so stopped to eavesdrop.

Adrie was indeed in a coma.

She interrupted and asked in Dutch which room Adrie was in. She just wanted to drop off some flowers, holding up the flowers she had.

Juul was nice enough to show her the way. Her friends were all very concerned and just didn't understand how Adrie could have a stroke, she was so health conscious. They suspected it was bought on by the death of her husband so recently, a true love story. Dahlia was unable to get a word in by the time they got to the door. She looked at Adrie, very peaceful in the bed. Will had noticed Dahlia going somewhere with some Dutch women so decided to tag along. Looked like she was onto something. Dahlia went in with the women and put the flowers in a vase next to her bed. She did it so well, like she knew Adrie.

Her and Juul had a bit of a longer conversation before Dahlia said her goodbyes and walked out. She motioned for Will to follow her and the two went to another waiting room further up the hall.

"Looks like we are busy for this arvo," he grinned.

"Well," Dahlia said with a concerned look. "You have some explaining. Apparently she was dropped off by some stranger in a black Audi with an Australian accent. You or your friend?"

"Ah yeah, that," Will said, already guilty.

"So why are we here?" Dahlia said.

"Truthfully, just wanted to make sure she was alright. I have some problems in my life that means I don't want the police involved. Doesn't mean you stop caring just because that's the case." Will amazed even himself.

Dahlia gave him a big hug. "I will go and ask at the nurses station. Juul will vouch for me."

Will could have kissed her.

Will returned home later that night nothing short of exhausted with news that Adrie was alive and had suffered a rare mid cortex stroke. She would live, and they were fairly sure her stroke had not left any permanent damage.

Chapter Eleven

Just run

Eugene was relieved on hearing the news that Adrie would recover.

That was truly good news, but it didn't change his plan. It wasn't what had happened to Adrie, or its outcome that were his problem. It is how that linked him to Lem that would be the issue. So it was time to go.

As Eugene was distracted by other things and not paying attention to his messages, Daaisi reminded Eugene that the dream render had complete processing but had not been viewed yet and not been sent to the test subject. Eugene quickly advised to put it on hold until he advised otherwise. He stopped and looked at the image. Adrie would be happy when she woke up as the angle had changed and you could clearly see Amber sitting astride a very happy Douglas.

Eugene had been busy making preparations. He began to pack the Range Rover and found much of the dream interceptor and associated tools fit perfectly in the roof box he had installed previously. He also had a small Engel travel fridge, a side mounted shade cover and had camping equipment for two. He and Paige had done a few outdoor adventures early on and he had hoped such days would be back again so had kept everything in good order.

Key to Eugene's plan would be to leave the dream bakery looking like things were still happening. He set several power use functions for the lights, heating, robot vacuums, appliances and some power fluctuations for the fridge. If

ANDREW THURLOW

they checked the power bill it would look like someone was still in residence. Communication was easy as Daaisi could take care of that, he did have his Satellite service that he could setup anywhere and a sat phone he could turn on in emergencies, hopefully it wouldn't come to that.

Will was in the interview room packing up his roller suitcase. He had been pushing all morning to get as much alcohol in the car as he could.

"We are going to need it for those cold nights. Camping is not as fun here as it was when we were kids," he barked.

Eugene had calculated, if they just did normal days driving and camped up at night, it was three days to Bulgaria. Hopefully that was all they would need as that was still within the EU zone so no hard checkpoints. Certainly no records kept of travellers I.D's. From there, they should have a few days extra provisions to accommodate the need to hang around on Bulgaria for a while while they found the best route over the Black Sea to Georgia. Otherwise they would have to go through Turkey where border checkpoints are a little tighter and if they are detained, things a little tougher to get out of. If they had to go to Turkey any excess alcohol would also have to be ditched.

From Georgia they could head inland to Azerbaijan or further into Turkmenistan, Tajikistan or Pakistan. Then into Asia. All of those places were unlikely to respond to any European calls for Eugene to be returned especially if the right palms were greased. He could easily monitor the situation and know whether it was time to look for a different identity, he doubted it, but better to be out of the way.

It made little difference but he would travel on his Australian passport to match Will who only had the one. The two of them could pass off as a couple of rich guys doing some travel until something better presented itself.

He had regular provisions delivered to the dream bakery so he didn't need to go out and just packed dry goods and food that was easy to store. They could pick up fresh fruit, vegetables and meat along the way.

Eugene had a pretty good supply of cash. Euros, US dollars, Pounds and even some Swiss Francs. He packed it all. He really didn't want to leave anything in the dream bakery that looked suspect and cash was definitely that.

"I'm set," Will said presenting his roller. "How are you going?" he asked Eugene.

"Yeah, everything required is ready, just need to get through this thing with Paige." he said thoughtfully.

"How did you want to do that?" Will asked. "I can wait here."

"That was option one. Option two says we drive up together and go from there. Option three says we pick a spot in transit and you can sit with the car."

"Or in a bar," Will slipped in.

"Unlikely," Eugene said. "You are bound to create or attract trouble," he smiled at Will.

Truth be told Eugene was looking forward to this. Rotterdam had been good to him, but it had been the place of some pretty poor memories of late. The problems with Paige, and the death of Lem.

He felt if he didn't move on something worse was going to strike, or his past was going to catch up with him.

Paige had chosen the restaurant in the Kimpton De Witt across from Centraal Station.

'Did she do that on purpose?' He wondered.

The two of them had stayed there a few times. Once, the most magical, was in a suite which had a balcony that looked out over the rooftops of Amsterdam. The suite felt like it was stolen out of a Disney castle, decked with soft pastel blues and whites.

"I think it's best I catch the train for the last bit," he said. "Otherwise we could get stuck in traffic and might not get out until late. Then we can aim to get south of Bonn into the middle Rheine, good camp sites in there around the Nurburgring."

"How about you head to Hilversum in the east. I can do what I need to do and you can meet me at the station and we can carry on."

"Is that option four?" Will joked.

"Sort of option three. Let's call it option 3a."

"Lets do it." Will replied with bravado. "3a."

"Give me five minutes," Eugene said and headed upstairs.

Eugene took a last look around the dream bakery. Pondering it might be his last.

***

Paige was nervous.

She had dressed to impress so felt confident in her appearance. She didn't feel quite so confident that she would make it through this conversation without breaking down. She wanted to have confidence in him, he only ever lifted her up.

She didn't make the call half heartedly, she had soul searched deeply before deciding to reach out to Eugene. But somehow she had to tell him she didn't want to be in Rotterdam. She had worked out some kind of fairy tale that he would follow her home like a puppy dog. She knew that was highly unlikely as he had already tried that once but she also knew he had a way of developing alternative plans lightning fast that would take into account all scenarios and everyone's requirements. She just needed to be honest.

Lets face it, that was the tough bit.

She had arrived early at the De Witt and ordered a coffee. She loved this place, it was one of the dreamy places Eugene would take her, places she felt like a princess or a queen or a movie star. He had taken her to some fantastic destinations, grand old castles, futuristic towers, rustic secluded cabins and beach wonderlands.

The destinations weren't the key. It was the other worldly aspect of being there. The distance it put between the reality of handling multiple marketing accounts for people who seemed the think it was something of a menial task to people treating you like you were someone special. That went double when she was with Eugene, he made her feel special beyond compare.

"How's the coffee beautiful," he said coming from behind her.

"Nowhere near as heavenly as yours," she replied rising to embraced him warmly.

He was obviously taken aback. Not expecting physical intimacy this early. She could see in his eyes that he had missed those hugs.

"Wow," he said. "A man could get used to those."

She smiled. He was always so appreciative of her. The waitress had seen the embrace and had waited patiently for the moment to pass.

"Can I get you something sir," she asked Eugene.

"I'll have an espresso, thank you." He replied, and took his seat opposite Paige.

He looked up and gripped her eyes in a slow burning, loving embrace.

"I have missed you beautiful. Tell me, what's been happening in your life? What brings you to Amsterdam?"

"I'm here to see you, of course," she replied. "I would have come to Rotterdam, but I do love this place." She motioned to what he thought meant the De Witt but may have been Amsterdam in general.

"Yes," he said."Good memories. Seems like yesterday you were dancing in the hail storm."

"I am still a little bit lost as to why that ended." She said almost tearing at the thought. "My life has turned into a shambles wrapped in confusion. My boss recently died just to get away from me, strange people say stranger things to me and I just find myself going around in circles trying to impress people who I think don't care about me at all."

"Oh." Eugene said, he was not expecting that.

Eugene's face showed he clearly had no expectations from this conversation today. She supposed he had thought through many scenario's, the worst was that she never spoke to him again, so they were already passed that. Paige chatted spontaneously, as was her way. Idea's popped into her head, mixed with feelings, emotional insights and intuitions. She was a clouded conundrum that, particularly as it had been over a year since they had spoken, let everything out. Thoughts she had been thinking, words she had spoken, people she had seen, feelings she had held back.

The coffee came and was consumed. Lunch was ordered but neither of them were here for eating so it was picked at but remained unfinished. They both knew that if lunch ended, this conversation would end and then they would go their separate ways again to what unknown end.

Eugene had obviously seen a moment to interject and asked. "So you think a homeless person on a train told you to come back to see me?"

She had mentioned that incident about twenty minutes ago but Eugene had a patient way of filtering the emotions and looking for the underlying meaning. Often, in Paige's outbursts, the end of the sentence or the conclusion of the paragraph didn't signal the end of the thought. Her thoughts weren't structured in that way or structured at all, they just arrived. Similarly, the start of a new totally separate thought still didn't conclude a previous thought. In truth all thoughts were jumbled up and expelled at a great rate followed by a reckoning, or possibly a further expulsion. He had told her before he felt her thoughts were like the spores of mushrooms with the results looking for a moist place to germinate. If such a place was found, a conversation might be possible if not there is always the next wave. It was an endearing feature and especially to someone with a memory such as his, not a hindrance.

"More confirmed it," she replied. "You know," she said the last part moving to a higher pitch in a way that must have melted his heart.

He did appear to know.

"A lot of things in my life seemed to have not turned the way I expected. The way they were when we were together was a dream." she stopped talking and reached out to hold his hand.

"When those dreams turned, what could I do? It's taken me a year and those dreams still haunt me."

"Yes," he said. He looked at her like he knew.

"Sorry to rush this." Eugene said. He looked like he wanted to listen more but had a time limit and had to get on with it. "I have been continuing my dream research but things have taken a very bad turn."

"First one of my subjects died. To protect my research I covered it up, it looks like I did this successfully but then another one had a stroke, just a few days ago. She is alive but I am going to have to make some plans to ensure what I have done goes underground for a while and I can't be found."

Paige stared at him aghast.

"You don't need to know anymore if you don't want," he said giving her a way out.

"It's okay," she replied. "Tell me."

"I need to get out of Holland and I would say best to get out of the EU. The only reason I haven't already gone is you being here. Nothing in the world is more important to me than you, but I think we need some time to work this out properly, otherwise I would say come with me now."

Eugene appeared to pause. Was he hoping she would agree and come with him now. Paige couldn't do that, she had pillars that kept her stable. Things in her life, that without, she would crumble. Her family mostly, but other pillars included her friends, her routine and her relationship. An unstable pillar would lead to an unstable Paige.

"Yes," Paige could now see that the puppy was not going to follow her home.

"I just need something from you," he asked earnestly.

"Of course," she said.

"If anyone contacts you. I need you to deny any contact with me recently or any knowledge of any dream research. I need you to say you had nothing to do with my work and as far as you know I do market research for financial companies."

"But Eugene," she said. "You're all over the Internet."

"Not for long," he said confidently. "The Internet has a short memory."

"I don't want to say much more. We need to keep talking, beautiful. There is so much more I need to say. So much I need to hear. But right now I need to go."

"Yes. I do to. Train back to London is in twenty five minutes," she said swallowing her pride hard.

∗∗∗

Eugene arrived at Hilversum just after three.

149

Will was waiting in the car park of the train station. He was very bored and was playing Rage against the Machine's Killing in the Name of very very loud.

Eugene moved him over and took the drivers seat.

"I should have thought of this before but we need to have phones off. We will pick up some burners along the way. I have a few ways you can get access to your messages and emails without letting anyone know where you are. I will set them up tomorrow. I know a place near Frankfurt I can get some tech."

"Turned off and in the glove box," Will said turning to get a Grolsch from the Engel." You're driving, I shall relax" he said smiling.

"Any water in there?" Eugene asked.

"Oh," Will had not put any water in the fridge. "Some in the back, it will be cold enough."

Eugene got out of the car and went to the back to get a bottle of water. He took a deep breath, was this a big mistake. Shouldn't he go after Paige, none of this mattered. A year ago, she walked out and now when she walked back in, he was running away. Eugene opened the bottle and took a big swig of water. He felt very drained. This would be different he concluded. When she walked out a year ago she put up shutters and blocked him out. He was getting out now to find a new life, hopefully for both of them, if she could come around to that. She had just told him that she missed him and wanted him back.

His estimation was, if it was real, then things would work out. He would keep communication going and listen to her better, that's what she needed.

Eugene started the drive down the A1 and made good time until the road became the A30 which then became the A12. By the time he hit the Autobahn the sun had started to descend, the two kept quiet for much of the journey.

Eugene was lost in his own thoughts and Will in the music and a few beers.

They camped in style on the outskirts of Bonn just off the Autobahn. Will was keen for a big drinking session but Eugene was still a little lost in his thoughts. He also had one mind on the drive the next day which was mostly left to him as Will was not going to be in any fit state. The two made Croatia late in the day and camped outside Zagreb.

Eugene was exhausted having taken the majority of the drive for the day. Will was still a little hungover and the two turned in early ready for the day tomorrow. The following day Will drove the majority through Serbia and into Bulgaria. They made Burgas late and setup quickly in a campsite near the ferry terminal.

Still feeling the effects of three days in the car the next day Eugene went to secure a ferry ride to Georgia, so far everything went without a hitch but there was a way still to go. He managed to secure the journey and as suspected the ferry terminal was paper based so the records taken were just written in a book. It would take a while before anyone discovered where they made their exit from Europe, if ever. The ferry journey took a few days and finally the two could relax a little, a few drinks and good food.

They arrived in Georgia early morning and after changing some cash for local currency got straight on the road for the drive to Azerbaijan. Eugene had made contact with a friend from his less salubrious past to help them cross the border without using their passports. He knew it would cost him dearly but it was a small price to pay for anonymity.

The agent met them in a roadside outside Tiblisi and drove with them to the border post in Vakhtangisi where he arranged for smooth passage through the check point. At Eugene's request the guard had also supplied some papers for them to show, if they were stopped anywhere else. It gave them a free reign in Azerbaijan without the need to reach for Australian passports, but the guard was clear that they shouldn't test the paper as it's content was as thin as it's substance. The two pushed on and made Baku after dark where Eugene had organised a villa for them to stay on the Caspian Sea Beach.

There was no drama to speak of on the journey, but an apprehensive fire grew in Eugene the further they went. A state of flux of his own making, questions unanswered and people chasing him for the results of his poorly executed actions, however well intended.

Will was clearly just enjoying the road trip but Eugene knew he needed to right the wrongs of this phase of his life.

Chapter Twelve

Epilogue

The day had been such a good one for Wim.

Three dockside gangsters taken down for a daylight bashing. His task force at the centre of making considerable progress in the cleaning up of Rotterdam's gangland. It was a big fight but he felt good for his part in it.

The coffee at the station hadn't improved and he poured the remaining contents of his cup into the sink and refreshed it from the pot. He really didn't like the filter coffee but it was supplied so he drank it in silent sufferance.

"Excuse me Detective Hummel," the officer was young, perhaps just out of the academy.

"Yes," Wim replied.

"I was wondering if I could bother you for a moment regarding a case you worked on prior to taking on the organised crime unit."

"Sure, which one." Wim was regularly asked for input. He didn't mind, it kept his hand in.

"The case I have is a woman who was delivered anonymously to a hospital. Regular follow up found she had been attending some marketing session at a dream bakery in Struisenberg.

Wim put down the ugly coffee changing his stance to show he was now intently engaged.

"Yes," he said resolutely. "I was sure there was something strange going on there but just couldn't nail it down. Some shifty Australians."

Wim took the case file from the junior and scanned it's contents.

"Adrie Winters had a stroke in the posterior cingulate cortex. Which is considered very uncommon."

"Can you pull the file of Lem Forth from the archive. I had some suspicions his death was not exposure but there was insufficient evidence. For my memory there was something peculiar around an uncommon stroke he also suffered."

"If the two strokes are the same we should present this to the boss and investigate further into the dream bakery."

"Serial Killer?" The junior officer questioned, wide eyed.

"Well technically one death doesn't make a serial killer." Wim corrected him.

"But we are onto something."

www.ingramcontent.com/pod-product-compliance
Lightning Source LLC
Chambersburg PA
CBHW022155260626
47155CB00018B/2049